Wall of Fire

Terrace VII

Wall of Fire

Purgatorio Towers #7

Sarah L. Johnson
& Robert Bose

Graphics and Cover Design
Emily Pratt & Aaron Bilawchuk

THE SEVENTH TERRACE
CANADA

Terrace VII: Wall of Fire

Robert Bose & Sarah L. Johnson — First Edition

Copyright © 2019 The Seventh Terrace

The Seventh Terrace
41 Mt. Yamnuska Place SE
Calgary, Alberta Canada T2Z 2Z6
www.the-seventh-terrace.com

Graphics and Cover Design by Emily Pratt & Aaron Bilawchuk

Loud as a Murder ©2015 originally published in *Crossed Genres 2.0 #28, April 2015*

ISBN 978-1-9992001-0-7

For the Hot Tub

— the start and undoubtedly the end —

of everything.

Contents

Dear Tenants,

What a year it's been at Purgatory Towers! I wouldn't say time has flown by – we are in limbo after all, LOL – but our community has seen significant changes. Exterior repairs are well underway after the Spring acid rains, the outdoor poet pit is now fully salted and ready for use, and we've had several new arrivals to the seventh floor.

I'd like to address the latter, due to the number of inquiries asking why, if suites are available, are lower level tenants not granted right of first ascension? Well, if I may be blunt, you all know why. As is set forth in the *Libro Purgatorium,* souls travel an infinite number of paths to arrive at the Tower where they are assigned accommodation, each according to their sins. Remember my friends, diversity is our strength! Each tenant is a uniquely corrupted snowflake, ascending at their own pace. Don't compare the stains on your soul to those of others.

Also worth noting, the Seventh Terrace, contrary to rumor, is not merely a darkened den of orgiastic delights. Whether you arrive through traditional ascension or vertical integration, there's suffering to be done. It's a Wall of Fire, folks. Walking through it is not going to tickle.

Lust is the top floor for a reason. It cannot be reconciled. Lust must be purged in order to gain entry to the rooftop pool party of Earthly Paradise. Can you lower level tenants claim to be ready for that? Most of us rather enjoy our carnal desires and are not prepared to consign them to the flames. Full disclosure: my Factory contract requires me to inform you that I do feed off this particular sin, but self-interest aside I'm only picking up what you're throwing down. Waste not, want not! On a related note, recycling and compost bins have been relocated to the morning lava ponds due to raccoon activity.

In closing, I remind you that fulfillment is found in the journey, not the destination. So, for those experiencing Seventh Terrace envy, don't be in such a rush. Take time to smell the brimstone, dance through the night blooming tulips, and mingle your flesh with that of your neighbors. Be sure to give our new top floor tenants a warm Purgatory Towers welcome, and know that the flames await us all.

Infernally Yours,

Gary

President

Purgatory Towers Tenant's Association

Betty

Robert Bose & Sarah L. Johnson

She never smiled.

Digger knew she could. She had perfect crimson lips built for smiling, sculpted and full, designed to make everyone feel loved. There was honestly no reason for her not to smile. She just didn't.

Snuggling her head in a clean towel, he placed her in his lap and stared into her eyes. Aquamarine, what the sky in heaven must look like. The eyes of an angel.

"Hi Betty," he said, smiling *his* best smile.

She didn't answer. That was okay. They shared their alone time in near silence, the background hum of dishwashers keeping them company. He snapped on a pair of green nitrile gloves and dabbed blobs of antibacterial soap on her cheeks. With a soft sponge he began rubbing in concentric circles, washing away the last traces of her latest lover. An asshole. They were all assholes, her lovers. He knew it. She knew it. No complaints from her though, she wasn't the complaining type. She just took it, never saying anything. Never smiling. Leaving him to clean up the mess.

When he had her face glowing, he slid a finger across her lips and into her mouth, producing a gush of semi-congealed slime. Digger held up his finger to the light and noted the consistency, sniffed it. Beyond being an asshole, the guy hadn't got off in ages; it was way, way past expiry. A boomer in all likelihood, probably dying of cancer. Digger definitely got a cancer vibe.

A chime went off letting him know he had another lady incoming. He slid two fingers into her mouth this time, extracted her slime filled oral cavity, and placed it on a mat next to her other orifices.

Another chime.

"Always a rush," he muttered, the spell broken. He reattached her head to her buffed, lustrous body, and inserted fresh orifices. The soiled ones went into the dishwasher set on warm and gentle. Not optimal, but he didn't have the time to clean twenty sets a shift by hand.

The conveyor grunted to life, belt crawling through a steel framed opening in the wall. This was Digger's clean room. His sanctum. None of the other brothel employees were permitted inside – not that any were exactly eager to intrude on what Fern called the 'wet work' – the vast majority of communication done wordlessly through the wall.

Another chime. The rubber curtain covering the hole parted as a large plastic bin slid through onto his receiving table. Digger popped off the lid and found Britney, a silicone brunette, folded in the customary fetal position. Tucked behind her legs were a pair of disembodied Feet with vaginas molded into the heels. The Feet dripped as he lifted them out. Artfully rendered, but with terrible vaginas. Non-removable. Hard to clean. And always damn filthy owing to the stiff construction and excessive depth. Clients tended to empty the lube bottle into them. The Feet were notoriously derided by his industry friends on the Scrub.

Digger always took care to sanitize the Feet thoroughly. Like Betty, the Feet were thermoplastic elastomer. As long as you kept it clean and oiled, no problem, but TPE was porous. An improperly cleaned orifice could grow terrible things.

Digger rubbed his slimy gloved fingers together and peered at them. Slick. Too slick. Silicone.

"Oh, no..." He tossed the Feet into the prewash tub and raced back over to the bin, lifting Britney out and carrying her quickly to the stainless steel bathing table. Clicking on the gooseneck lamp, he gently brushed dark hair out of her thick-lashed sable eyes. "Show me where it hurts."

Meticulously, he poured over every inch of her body with a microfibre cloth, wiping away any trace of the lubricant that would eat away her tender skin. Like dissolved like, and silicone lube was acid on a silicone doll. House rules clearly stated that clients use only the water-based lubricant provided. Digger's breath stormed in his lungs and he sealed his lips shut lest it escape in a howl. Not Betty, thank bleach. Not Betty... but not no one. He turned her over for a crevice check. Not only did he find a lot more silicone lube laced with milky threads of semen, but also a single cigarette burn on her plug-in anus.

"Fern," Digger gasped as the elevator doors opened and he barged into his boss's open concept office on the top floor.

"Digger?" Fern looked up from the three twenty-seven-inch monitors arrayed on his desk. "Namaste."

Digger slowly inhaled the funk of marijuana, sandalwood, and bare feet. While he'd only worked at Ahimsa Lotus Garden less than a year, he'd done time in a lot of other brothels, cleaned a lot of toys, and he'd never had a boss quite like Fern. For one thing, Fern was polite, relaxed, and didn't yell. Digger did not care for hostile work environments, so he liked Fern, even if he wore pants made of yarn, reeked of tea tree oil, and was probably not actually named Fern.

"Sorry to interrupt."

Fern clicked his mouse a few times and stood. "No worries, buddy. Door's always open, you know that." He gestured to the cluster of enormous hemp cushions that served as a seating area centred around a low platform with a stick of smoking incense and an ashtray dotted with several roaches.

"It's one of the dolls. She came back—"

"Sit," Fern insisted, picking up a teapot and two ridiculously tiny cups. "Take some tea."

"I don't—"

"We'll send our roots into the earth."

"We're on the fifth floor."

"And once grounded, open our hearts and shine our truth."

This was why Digger avoided talking to co-workers. He flopped into one of the cushions and Fern poured the tea, fingernails and knuckle creases packed with red clay from his weekend pottery retreats. It was all Digger could do not to recoil when Fern settled cross-legged with his own tea cup, soles of his feet blackened, like he'd walked to work barefoot.

Digger took a perfunctory slurp of tea.

Fern grinned. "Illuminating, right? Night Blooming Tulip. Ethical trade and certified fruitarian."

It tasted like mold, something left to fester and die and come back to life. But Fern wasn't asking his opinion, so Digger didn't give it.

"What's got your chakra's out of alignment?" Fern asked.

Digger reached into his pocket and dropped the silicone anus beside the teapot. He'd cleaned the part, but no amount of TLC could erase the burnt crater on the rim.

Fern stared at the anus. Digger stared at Fern.

"Digger, I know how you feel about—"

"It's abuse."

"I'll handle this."

"You mean you'll ban him."

"Let's not overreact."

"He used silicone lube."

Fern picked up the orifice, stretched it open and sling-shot it into the organics pail beside his desk. "So we bill his credit card for a replacement b-hole. And for smoking in the room."

"Are you serious?"

"Wear and tear is expected, my man. You know that."

"This isn't wear and tear, it's sadism." Digger paused, tightly gathering the coarse upholstery in his fists. "He hurt her, Fern. He hurt her horribly, on purpose."

Fern brought his stained hands together in prayer pose, and breathed in and out of his nose, noisily.

"Fern?"

Fern held up a staying hand and repeated the sonorous nasal inhale and exhale a dozen times before opening his eyes. "It's called Ujjayi breathing. Expanding success. You ought to practice it. I'm going to a yoga and basket weaving retreat next month. If you're interested, you're welcome to share a yurt with me."

Digger shook his head. "I can't sleep in circular environments. You're really not going to do anything?"

"We already have." Fern sipped from his tea cup. "We've held space for a human being to fulfill their desire without judgment."

"So, you don't have a problem with your... property," Digger stumbled over the word, "being abused like this?"

"Consider the alternative. We all got a darkness inside. We all dream of doing things society and morality would never allow us to enact. Those desires build up, and unreleased transform into rage. Just imagine what this client might do to a human partner, were it not for our services providing an outlet? We're ethical hedonists, Digger. Pleasure without harm. It's healthier this way. Drink your tea."

Stunned, Digger drank. "Least it wasn't Betty."

"Pardon?"

"Uh, more tea?"

Fern poured Digger another, and he drank that too. Eventually, he stumbled back into the elevator and took the five-story slide with a bad taste in his mouth.

Back in his clean room, Digger booted up his laptop and logged into his favourite industry message board. If Fern wouldn't do anything about this monster, maybe his friends could help.

The live chat part of The Scrub was a virtual party twenty-four hours a day, seven days a week, bursting with slung innuendo, animated gifs, and various discussions relating to the care and feeding of every form of love-machine. These were Digger's people, his tribe, but not everyone took their responsibility seriously.

Case in point.

The third Thursday of every month, a bunch of them got together for nachos down at the Twisted Nipple. Why they insisted on meeting at a strip club eluded him. He'd gone once, and they'd laughed in horror when he'd ordered, and eaten, a platter of extra cheesy nachos while sitting in sniffer's row, with sweat drenched asses and tattooed tits inches from his face. The nachos were terrible. He hadn't gone back.

Not all the board regulars were like that. Over the years he'd made a number of excellent, dependable friends. One was online when he logged in.

Tikka blasted out a message before his screen even finished loading. "Good afternoon, Gravedigger."

Years back when he first joined the group, he'd been working strictly night shifts at a shop in Saskatoon and had a reputation for threatening to bury dreadful clients.

"Not good," he replied, pounding the keys of the waterproofed laptop hard enough to make them shriek.

"Need a shovel?"

"Maybe. Probably. Had a burner earlier. Asshole." He watched her avatar swap to an animated mass of probing mauve tentacles.

"Betty?"

"No… but still, you know?"

She sent a string of custom squid hug emoticons.

"It pisses me off, and Fern…"

"Doesn't care."

"You got it. Won't even consider a ban."

"Serious suckage. What'cha going to do?"

Digger eyed the time. Nearly 5pm. Fern would head home soon, so there'd be a window to paw, uninterrupted, through the customer files. "The usual, see if I can find the bastard's info and pass it around. I'd love to do more..."

"Just say the word, Dig, and all my tentacles are yours."

A chime signalled an incoming arrival to the clean room.

"Thanks, Tikka, one of these days I'm going to take you up on that."

Ahimsa Lotus Garden whored out a dozen Charity M69 sex dolls, customized with a variety of heads, skin colours, and technology packages. Digger remembered opening the shipping crates and unpacking the first of his wards, his breath torn away when he gazed in those bright blue eyes. A certain *Koi No Yokan*, as Tikka liked to say. They hadn't blinked until he'd charged them up, of course, but he'd felt the spark, the instant connection. He'd cared for a lot of ladies over the years, from the days of tin-cure mannequins and doll-shaped latex balloons. Nothing came close to Betty though, nothing.

Sure, the others were similar, like sisters, and during the occasional lull, when they sat in their recharging alcoves, they'd stare at him, the corners of their custom deep throat mouth units curling up, reminding him they weren't her. He kept Betty close, always the last one to go out unless a customer requested her, which, to his chagrin, was all too often. She was the best, and he wasn't the only one who knew it.

Tuesday nights were dead. Quiet. Digger didn't mind, it gave him time to catch up on cleaning and maintenance, and more importantly, extra time with Betty. He mopped and disinfected the bamboo hardwood Fern insisted brought a deep connection to the natural beauty of the business, and then ordered some food. Twelve hour shifts and shitty customers made him hangry. Four-cheese nachos with the works would fill the void, supplying all major food groups, regardless of what everyone said. When his work area was spotless, he turned down the lights and dragged a stool over to Betty's alcove. He unscrewed the lid of his company supplied BPA free aluminum water bottle and took a long drink.

"I think you'd love the ocean," he said, tucking her under a soft blanket. "Well, not swimming of course, the salt water would devour you. And you'd want to stay under an umbrella so the sun wouldn't bleach your skin, and sheltered so the wind wouldn't dry you out. But aside from that, you'd love it. Endless sand, waves, and sky."

Her eyes glittered in the light thrown from his laptop's screensaver.

"I'll bring you a picture tomorrow. We can hang it right here." He tapped a blank spot on wall plastered with pictures of exotic landscapes. "It'll make you smile, I promise."

Last call came in at 10 p.m. and Digger loaded up the ladies in their numbered bins, sending them out on the conveyor belt. His heart sank when he read the serial number on the last booking. Sending Betty out for last call meant he'd be gone by the time she came back. Betty didn't mind her job, and Digger had no objections either – honest work was honest work – but the idea of her returning to the clean room, soiled, used, stuffed in a dark bin for hours... He contemplated sending one of the other models in her place, one that looked similar, but if he did that and the client complained, Fern would have his head. Ahimsa's ethos was not only based around the Vedic virtue of non-violence, but also the idea of connection and consent. That dolls chose clients as much as clients chose the dolls. Digger wanted to dismiss it as a hemp-eating perversion of ancient philosophy, but he understood better than Fern the idea of spiritual connection.

"Duty calls, Betty," he said, gently lowering her into her bin. "I'll wait for you, okay? I've got something I need to do before I go."

The elevator seemed to take forever to sneak up to the fifth floor. When the doors finally slid open, Digger peered into the shadows, interrupted only by street light filtering through the windows.

"Hello?" Digger called, but his voice bounced off the bamboo bookshelves and the only reply was a soft trickle from the lotus pond water feature. The floor had a vacated energy, the musky human stench gone stale.

The monitors lit up when Digger jostled the mouse, and Fern never locked anything, thank bleach. Passwords were viewed as a lethal chakra blockage. The booking software was easy enough to find and Digger started clicking through entries. If they ever got audited it would appear as though they had a single client named John Smith with an omnipresent indefatigable hard-on for synthetic flesh. He backtracked to the burner's time slot and found John Smith's booking for the doll that came back damaged.

But the payment info field, normally providing credit card number along with legal name and address, was blank. Even if a client paid cash, a credit card pre-auth was required for "incidentals" (like a partially melted anus). How could there be no credit card on file?

"God damn it." Digger flopped back in the rattan chair stirring up a cloud of unwashed armpits. Fern probably purged the payment info, suspecting Digger wasn't satisfied. Probably didn't even bill the burner for damages, thinking Karma would provide its own retribution. So much for non-violence and consent. Fern didn't understand the first thing about Ahimsa.

Without a name there was nothing he could do. Time to call it a night. But first, he darted forward and clicked on the most recent booking.

Client Name: Smith, John

Companion: Charity M69-10 (Betty)

Digger clicked on the payment info tab.

…

Blank. He refreshed the page. Still blank.

"Betty," he whispered and the chair legs screeched across the floorboards as he launched towards the elevator, punching the basement level. "Come on, come on."

The old elevator grew hotter as it trundled down on greasy cables. Fern thought climate should be experienced authentically, but building code and ventilation standards said otherwise. So, Fern ran the A/C during business hours with the fans shutting down the minute the last client clocked out. And that meant one thing. Betty was back.

Digger's coveralls were clammy with sweat by the time the elevator opened into the clean room. Three bins waited on the receiving table. He ripped them open, flinging the lids on the floor. Barbara, Brooke... and the final fetal doll.

Burns, a line of them. Charred lesions dotted her flank, curving around her hip and disappearing down into her groin. A smear of rusty red on her thigh.

"Betty?" He reached in, peeling the befouled packing sheet away from her shoulders. He choked, as though an ogre's hands squeezed his throat. "No."

Betty's head was gone.

The dolls were heavier than one might expect, even headless, and when he heaved Betty up, one of her arms flopped over his shoulder. The reek of melted rubber overpowered his senses, and her hand lingered on his back, a gentle touch, as if assuring him, *it's okay, I'm okay.*

Well, it sure as hell was not fucking okay. Betty did not choose this.

"Tikka!" he wailed into the phone. "Fuck sakes, pick up. I can't... he hurt her... I need to... please help—" the beep cut him off, he redialed, got notification that the voicemail was full. How many messages had he left? Not that many. Surely not that many. He almost dropped the phone when it buzzed in his hand.

"What kinda psychopath blows up my phone by actually *calling* me?" Tikka snapped, her voice echoing over speaker.

"Did you check your messages?"

"Fuck no, only perverts leave voicemails—"

"It's Betty."

Tikka paused. "Tell me."

Digger laid it all out, pacing back and forth, wearing a trench in the concrete.

"Son of a fungus," Tikka growled. "Ah man, burners are a dime a dozen but the decapitation..."

"His info was purged, and I need to find this guy," Digger said. "Tikka?"

"Where are you?"

"Uh..." He stared up at the corrugated steel wall of the Factory realizing how deranged it would sound. "Right outside."

A moment later Tikka booted the door open. Clad in purple coveralls, tattoos emerging from her collar, vining up her throat and terminating at her chin, goggles perched on her tiny head, gloved hands up, glistening with viscous fluid. The closest thing to a friend Digger had in meat space. A meticulous custodian, no one knew more about the ins and outs of the industry than Tikka, and she took absolute zero shit from anyone.

Showing up in the middle of the night was not the most ingratiating approach.

"Get in, loser," she said, peering out the door and looking both ways. "Before Beef finds you loitering."

"Beef?"

"Our security."

"Your security guard's named Beef?"

She cocked her hip against the doorframe. "And you're in love with a TPE fuck-bucket. We all got quirks."

"Her name is Betty."

"Walk and talk, Digger," Tikka said, pivoting on one chunky heel and stomping down the cinder brick hallway.

He followed her into the warehouse, through plastic sheeting where her clean room was set up on a scale several times larger than his. She had an octopus the size of a mini-cooper on her table, two unblinking eyes in a bulbous head, algae green and black tentacles as thick as Digger's legs spiraling together in a great gloopy nest. With no hesitation, Tikka dove in, elbow deep.

"So, your guy," she said, vigorously milking an appendage. "The burning and the heads, I know that M.O."

"You got a name?"

"Got a lot more than that." She wrung the mayonnaise out of the last tentacle. "Lemme get the flush going. I don't have to tell you, the mould that can colonize in these things is practically sentient. Clients don't want to tangle with Lovecraft come to life."

Digger shifted foot to foot, winding and unwinding his fists, trying not to think about Betty, dismembered, as Tikka hooked the octopus up to a sanitizing machine capable of flushing every last trace of DNA out of the giant silicone beast. Then she stripped off her gloves, dropped them in the biohazard bin, went to her computer, and jotted something down on a post-it.

"I keep my own black list and this sounds like a client from my old work."

"The furry place? Or the one where clients pay to be tickled?"

She shook her head, glossy black hair slipping out of her pony tail. "The morgue."

"The… actual morgue?"

Tikka pursed her lips. "Not my proudest moment, okay? I was young and needed the money yadda, yadda. Anyway, this creep ain't content to politely get his rocks off with the unclaimed cadavers. He mutilated them."

Digger reached for the yellow note, but Tikka stepped back.

"Before I give this to you, I wanna know your intentions."

"Tikka, I don't have time."

"Make the time. I'm the voice of sober second thought here. You seem a tad red-shifted for someone planning nothing more than a good ol' fashioned doxxing."

Digger eyed the folded note. "I'm getting her head back. That's all."

Tikka gave him a dubious look and grazed her bare fingers along a tentacle, gently throbbing with the work of the flush machine. All Digger could think of was Betty's smile, and never getting a chance to see it.

"I know how much she means to you," Tikka said, stroking her pet monster. "People... they don't get us, do they?"

Digger shrugged. "We've got each other."

"Take it and scram," she said, pressing the note into his hand. "And Dig?"

"Yeah?"

"Not saying you need a sidekick, but I'm just putting it out there that I'm super-hot and ready for murder."

Digger couldn't remember the last time he'd hugged another human being, but he wrapped his arms around Tikka now, noting how all the bony structures in her tiny body poked at him in a way Betty never could. How she squeezed him back the way Betty never would. All those moving parts. If anything, he ought to be Tikka's sidekick, not the other way around.

"Be careful," she whispered. Then she shoved him back and once again gloved up, pulled her goggles back down over her face, and reached into a bin to pull out a rubber scorpion as big as she was. "See your own self out. And hit me up later... in text form."

Digger checked the address for a third time, gaping at the twin geodesic domes encircled by flower-choked ponds and ivy threaded brick walls. Not what he expected. It looked like two giant white breasts rising into the night sky. Definitely ugly enough to be some rich perv's dream home. He wiped a sweaty hand against his stained coveralls and tightened his grip on the tire iron. "I'm coming, Betty."

Darting through the open gate, he followed a path that led between the ponds. A frog croaked from a lily pad and he jumped, his sweat turning cold. He imagined the ponds were supposed to be calming, but he felt anything but. Anger smoldered inside. Rage even. Tikka asked what his intentions were. Betty and... he wasn't sure what, but he didn't like the thoughts oozing out of his mind like over-lubed Feet.

TERRACE VII: WALL OF FIRE

Hand shaking, he pushed the doorbell, shaped and painted to resemble a flower, or maybe a clit, and heard the faint notes of a pan flute. Waited. Mashed the button a couple more times. Nothing.

Someone was home. Someone had to be home.

On a whim he tried the door, almost annoyed to find it unlocked. For a moment he wondered what he'd do if this wasn't the right place. Tikka knew this guy years ago, he could have moved since. But it was too late for that, he slipped in and tugged the door closed behind him.

Standing in the opulent entry hall, Digger immediately knew he was in the right place. The walls were plastered with large frame nudes. Not tasteful ones either. Like blown up porno centerfolds tacked into glossy black frames. The grand chandelier, lovely at first glance, was a glittering mosaic of crystal penises. Instead of lions or dragons flanking the stairs, two white marble statues of downward dog posing women, asses stretched wide. He'd seen a lot of weird shit over the years, but this took the toy chest.

Digger didn't much like or trust rich people, especially ones with poor taste. They tended, as Fern had pointed out, to have darkness inside them. He bet

Fern loved this slimeball though, his darkness and his money, the perfect client, one able to pay for premium service without leaving any incriminating records.

"Hello," he called, loud enough to echo. "Anyone home?"

He nearly screamed when his phone buzzed, and fumbling, fished it out of his pocket. "Jesus, Tikka."

"Are you there?"

"Didn't you just chew me out for phoning you?"

"Don't get cute, you're at his place, aren't you?"

"It's like an eighties Hustler in here," he said. "With extra Larry Flynt."

"Holy shark shit, you broke in?"

"I tried ringing the bell."

"At 2 a.m. Are you nuts?"

"Betty's here, Tikka. I'm not leaving without her."

"Then you're keeping me on the horn. In case this plan of yours goes tits up."

He shifted the tire iron to his other hand, tucked the phone between his ear and shoulder and started exploring, each room more distasteful than the last, reporting the details to Tikka as he went. A pair of the Feet in the bathtub, bound up in red panties, oozing the Fungi from Yuggoth or some other cosmic horror.

An old blow up doll in a closet, partially deflated, gaping fish mouth gone slack. Throughout the house he noticed the grime, the neglect, the floor smudged with dirty footprints, light switches smeared with rusty red.

"This place is filthy."

"Whaddya expect from a pig?" Tikka replied.

"Not an eight-car garage." Digger followed a staircase into an underground garage, revealing a long line of luxury vehicles. A BMW, two Mercedes, a damn Bentley, and oddly, a beat-up VW minibus.

"If this guy is that rich, he's got security. You're probably on camera."

"Too late now." Digger slashed his tire iron through the windows of each and every one, not bothering to shield his face from the exploding glass. Searching the interiors, he found only the same cakey smudges of red, and pine forest air freshener so thick he could taste it.

"What the hell are you doing?" Tikka yelled.

"She's not in any of the cars," he replied, stomping out of the garage.

"You said you were just going to get her head back and now you've trashed a million dollars' worth of automobile, you maniac. You get pinched, they'll put you away for a hundred years."

"If I don't help her, who will?"

"Well consider this, Lancelot," Tikka snapped. "Betty never asked you to save her. She's not some damsel in distress."

"Tikka, I told you—" A heavy thump came through the ceiling above.

"Dig?"

"Someone's here."

Digger ran through the mansion, taking the stairs two at a time. "Betty," he yelled, "I'm here, I'm coming."

He kicked open a set of double oak doors. A waft of armpits and wet pennies slapped him in the face as he charged in, tripping over a pile of broken pottery, and breaking his fall on the Victorian four-poster, where his hands splashed into a dark warm puddle.

"What is it?" Tikka asked.

"A dead guy," Digger said, wiping his hands on the sheets and switching on the bedside lamp. He stared at the blood splashed body in a peacock print kimono.

"Recognize him?"

"His head is off," Digger said, but he knew. From the dirty soles of the feet and the red clay caked under the fingernails. And beneath the meaty stench of blood... tea tree oil. "It's Fern."

"The fuck—your hippy dippy boss is my old head hunter?"

"You were right, Tikka."

"Digger, this is serious shit, you need to get out of there, now."

"She saved herself." Digger reached across to the pillow next to the headless corpse, sweeping the blood-drenched hair out of her aquamarine eyes. Her angel's face was undamaged, thank bleach. He took a corner of the sheet and gently dabbed the blood from her smiling lips. "Hi, Betty."

Trace and Solomon
Go To Hell

Robert Bose

Trace pushed gore-splattered hair behind her ear and straightened the red ribbon around her neck, smile bent sinister.

"What did you do?" accused Solomon, dropping his cigarette and grinding it out.

She held up a sheet of parchment to the sun and squinted through it. "Fixed our problems."

"Shit," he said, glimpsing the watermark. "Is that?"

"Yeah." Trace thrust the sheet towards him, yelping as the wind tore it free, parchment dancing above the pavement.

"Jesus, woman." Solomon pinned it with his boot. "We're not that desperate."

"Are you fucking kidding me?" With a blood-smeared arm, she pointed at their old Winnebago, stained with age and falling apart. "We're skint. We have a tank of gas, a few hundred in change, half a bag of Dorito's, and bounty hunters on our ass. It's a goddamn opportunity, Sol."

Solomon stooped to snag the sheet, studying the eight-item list written in tight calligraphy. "Ever heard of anyone completing a contract from The Factory?"

"Well, no."

"That's because it's goddamn crazy. Only one place we can find most of this crap. But you know that."

"It'll get us off the game board for a while. Plus, it's fifty fucking grand." She slid her arms around him, pressing her head into his chest. "No regrets."

Her motto. Her mantra. Emblazoned across every crop top and every dress, even if he was the only one who could see it. God, he loved that, and her, even if it was a disaster most of the time.

He squeezed her with scarred arms, holding tight until she wriggled away. "Thought we were done with that shit hole."

"It's not that bad," she said. "Cheap, easy, and hot. Kinda like Cabo."

"And the deadline?" he asked, handing back the list.

"Twenty-four hours. Nineteen now, I didn't want to wake you."

"Asshole hunters aren't far behind. You thin the herd some?"

"They chose the wrong Circle-K for a late-night snack." She stretched her arms and spun away, slipping on a patch of Walmart parking lot gravel and catching herself on the motorhome's open side door. The hinges groaned and twisted. "Sounds like you. Not sure which is more old and busted."

"Bloody hell, I just fixed that." Sol shoved her inside, pinching her ass before turning his attention to the door, the aluminum still warped from that idiot cyclist. Hammering the hinges into alignment, he patted the side of the 76' D-23 Chieftain. He was older than the Chief, and debatably in worse shape. At least the Chief was vintage. Trace disappeared to the back and he picked up the coffee he'd poured when he woke up and realized she'd sneaked off during the night. He let the sludge warm in his mouth before forcing it down.

Music filtered from the bedroom, Trace singing along with some crap tune as she cleaned herself up. Must be new. Newer. Then again, if it wasn't eighties rock, who knew what the fuck it might be. He started the Chief and pulled onto the highway, mentally mapping out a route to the nearest crossroads.

Warm hands landed on his shoulders, fingers finding purchase and thumbs digging in.

"Tight," she said, pressing hard enough to make him hiss. "You're one big knot. That hurt?"

"Yes."

"Want me to stop."

"Never."

Her breath curled around his ear, mint with a hint of bourbon, carrying a rhyme.

"Collected hearts

And other parts

The keys to many doors

Though consider this

Beyond a kiss

I never collected yours."

"Is that poetry? I figured —"

Her hand snaked around, covering his mouth. "No."

"Right…"

"Not another word, you." Her other hand caressed his throat.

He kept his next retort to himself and nibbled her fingers, tasting soap and hand cream, heard his stomach rumble.

"Stop that," she barked. "Now you're making me hungry."

"Where'd that bag of Doritos end up?"

"I ate the Doritos."

"What?" He bit harder. "Cruel, maybe I'll eat you."

"Promises, promises. I'm serious about being hungry though. I'm fucking starving."

"You had time to grease a few bounty hunters at the Circle K, but didn't think to grab some groceries?"

"Please, like this is my first day?" She retreated into the back, whispering fragments of her not-poem, rummaging through her big purse.

"Tell me you didn't rob the place."

"Jesus Sol, relax. The mess I left, ain't nobody noticing a few missing sandwiches, annnd..." She handed him a wrapped square. "Banana bread. Fresh."

Peeling away the wrap, he took a bite and moaned. "Perfect."

"Am I going to groan like that when I'm your age?"

"Yep."

"Then I better not."

"Make noises?"

"Get old." She leaned in, taking a big bite out of his banana bread before unwrapping her own. "As long as I outlive you, at least by a few seconds."

Back on the highway, Trace reclined her seat and curled up in a ball, dozing for a few hours. She looked so small, so fragile, and so beautiful. Solomon loved every inch of her. Except that damn ribbon. He could give it a little tug, pull the threads and watch it float away, but then she'd be gone. Or he'd be dead. Or both.

She stirred awake when Def Leppard's "Animal" came on and he cranked up the volume.

"I had the dream again," she yawned.

"About the five of us?"

"Cannonball Run."

"You like that dream."

She cracked a Red Bull and chugged it, her burp overpowering the blaring speakers. "We never get to the end though, there's always something."

"Right," he said. Always something.

"Still hungry?"

"Yeah, hand me a sandwich."

"Don't think a ham and cheese is going to cut it," she said, pulling her dress over her head and tossing it behind the seat. Red panties and bra followed.

"Hold on, give me a—"

She bounced onto his lap and straddled his knee, ramming her left nipple into his eye the exact moment he pulled out to pass a dawdling Prius. A horn screamed and he yanked the wheel hard to avoid colliding with an extra-wide fish truck.

"Jesus Christ, woman."

"Calling me God, already?" she said with a moan, grinding against his thigh.

He wiggled to see more of the road. "This was a hell of a lot easier with Choncey driving."

"He came a long way from where we found him. Passed out in the ladies', naked except for this ribbon around his neck. He came to love us."

"You, maybe." Sol ran his tongue around her nipple.

"Mmm. He said he was French."

Sol laughed, almost choking. "Well, wouldn't you? Belgians... Jesus. I don't miss his taste in music though, Hank Williams and Olivia Newton John."

37

"You love ONJ."

"One song. One goddamn song." Sol caught the sign he'd been waiting for and turned off the highway, cranking the wheel with one arm, the other still tight around Trace's waist. "Show time. You might want to toss a little something over those bones."

Running her fingers through his hair, she let her lips skip down his cheek and nipped his neck. "By my reckoning, we have five miles. No hurry." A cigarette appeared from behind her ear. "Where'd you stash your Zippo?"

"You're sitting on it."

"Ah, I figured—"

"Yeah, yeah." He reached down between her legs into his sopping pocket, lit her up, plucking the cigarette from her hand after she'd taken a long drag. "Why do you insist on stealing Virginia Slims?"

"Why not? You've come a long way, baby." She snatched the Slim back, puffed it down and flicked the butt out the window. Dug through her hair for another one. "Hmm, must have escaped."

"Happens. It's hungry again."

"Voracious." She shook her head, curls pouring over her shoulders and into his face.

He swung her around. "Pest. We'll be there in a couple. Get your sweet ass in gear."

She made a face and rolled off, grabbing his crotch and letting her fingers trail across his hip before darting out of sight.

At least he still had a few moves she couldn't match. Yet. He popped her missing cigarette into his mouth. Menthol, yuck, but easier than remembering where the hell he'd left his Reds.

"I saw that, beast!" Her voice echoed from the back.

The gravel road intersected a traffic circle surrounding a spike of weathered black granite. Solomon rolled the Chief onto a patch of goat-chewed grass shaded by twisted oaks and headed to the back of the motorhome, kicking off damp pants and boxers. Trace tossed him a pair of jeans as he hopped down the velvet upholstered aisle.

"Thanks, darling." He opened a closet door and pulled out an olive-green ammo box. Tossed it on the bed. "Seen my Mossberg kicking around?"

"Which one?"

"The Shockwave."

"Third drawer, behind the lube."

Sol pulled out the shotgun, loaded it. Slipped on a shoulder holster and tucked in his 1911. "Ready?"

She lifted her scarlet sundress, flashing black panties and a Herstal FNP-9 strapped low on her thigh. "Always. Now put your pants on, or is your strategy to beguile our host with mismatched socks, t-shirt, and a donkey dick?"

"It crossed my mind."

"I dare you." She danced past him, kicking the door open to disappear outside.

Sol found a clean'ish pair of boxers, the ones with the penguins, and tugged on his jeans. Stuffed the Mossberg into his bulging gear duffel, pausing to add a crumpled piece of paper he extracted from under the mattress. Tricky writing, done in secret. She'd hate it, but he owed for her the twisted rhyme she'd blown in his ear.

He caught up with her in front of the granite marker, hands on her hips.

"Feels like ages."

His lips brushed the back of her neck. "Our first adventure. I remember you drank that entire jug of Zoroastrian Haoma and tried to have sex with the wall."

"That was a trip. I loved that wall."

"And it loved you. How's our time?"

The parchment came out of her bra and she held it up to the sun. "Thirteen hours."

"Plenty." He kissed her again and headed back to the Chief. "I'll get a bucket, tag one of those goats in the field over there, and we'll get this party started. We can get everything from the Bazaar with a bit of bartering and still make Denver by tomorrow."

"Hold up. There's an easier way."

He turned back. "That is the easier way. You remember the hard way, don't you? We pay the farmer down the road a *special* visit."

"Things have changed darling, a bucket of blood, human sacrifice? That's so old school." Trace pulled her phone from her handbag, fiddled for a second before grunting and swiping right with an exaggerated flick of a finger. "Sweet. I need a little of your A negative though."

Sol raised his eyebrows and trudged back, digging a butterfly knife out of his back pocket. He flicked it open and sliced his thumb, reached up to plant a print against the stone.

"On the phone, silly." She grabbed his hand and mashed it against the screen, leaving a long smear.

Examined her handiwork. "Perfect. Shouldn't take long."

An app? Jesus. Times *were* changing. He stuck his oozing thumb in his mouth and wiped the blade on his thigh. Spun it around his finger a few of times before it slipped off and clattered to the gravel.

Trace kicked him in the ribs when he bent to pick it up. "Stop being old."

"Stop being a pest. Oh wait, you can't." He grabbed her foot and shoved her on her ass, watching her tanned knees splay open as she flopped back, still holding her phone to her face. "Who are we waiting for? Mephistopheles?"

"The current incarnation at least."

"Really? I liked the old one, he was a character. That, uh, app say what happened to him?"

"Retired. Apparently. Moved to the Sixth Circle, built a McMansion in a fancy part of Dis."

"You're shitting me."

"Of course. Who the fuck knows what happens to those monsters, he probably choked on a baby or something. All I know is there's a shiny gold badge next to his name."

A loud whine cut the air and a white Porsche Cayenne materialized out of a billowing red dust cloud, tearing around the circle and throwing a wave of gravel against the Chief's siding.

"Definitely not Meph. This fucker requires a lesson on manners," said Sol, pushing his duffle open with a toe.

"Chill." Trace patted his shoulder and walked towards the SUV. "Just a new guy entrance. You know, a three-point superhero landing."

The Cayenne's door opened and a young man got out, lit a cigarillo, and smiled at Trace. Everything about him, from his boat shoes and creased chinos to his preppy sweater vest, feathered hair, and golden tan, screamed old money frat boy. Of course, it was just a thin façade over some horrific denizen of Hell. It never failed though, even the civilized ones looked like Republicans.

"You called, fair lady? Mephistopheles at your service." he purred, giving her a half-bow. "But call me Flea."

Sol scoffed and Trace shot him dark look.

"Nice to meet you Flea. Don't mind my partner, he's an old fart."

"I see that." The demon blew out a cloud of smoke far greater than any human lungs could produce. "So, what can I do for you? Fame? Fortune? Want to take a different fork in your recent past?"

"Nothing so grand. We need a day pass to the Bazaar."

"That, I can't help with unfortunately, The Gates of Hell are strictly off limits to the living at the moment. The Prince of Lies—"

"Doesn't give a rat's ass," Sol and Trace said at the same time.

Flea held up his hands, palms out. "Look, the rules have changed. Do you know what happens to living souls if they die in Hell? Of course you don't. It's... indeterminate at best. Never used to be problem, since the living never wanted to go there. But, in the last few years it got trendy for the well-heeled and well-versed to cozy up to the Gates, spend a night and catch a bite one foot from eternal torment. Inevitably, idiots found ways to get killed. At the start it wasn't a big deal, like who cares about one or two missing souls, but soon it was dozens and then hundreds." He took a long drag and released another cloud. "Messed up the ethereal balance or something. So, yes, Lucy does care and it's a no-go, out of my hands."

"Fuck," said Trace, turning to look at Sol. "We need to get there, I signed that Factory contract in blood. We have half a day and change to fulfill the terms or…"

"A Factory contract? You two are fucking crazy. Nobody ever gets the last item on those," said Flea. "It's rigged."

"Yes," said Sol, reaching into his duffel and pulling out a long obsidian dagger.

The demon took a step back and turned to run, almost reaching his car door before the thrown blade caught him in the back. He slid down the white paint, leaving a midnight stain.

"Now," growled Sol, stomping over, "let's start over. We need a pass to the Bazaar. For free, mind you, on account of you wasting our amazingly precious time."

Flea thrashed in an expanding pool of ichor, trying to reach the dagger, his careful illusion flickering to show his true form: a writhing, crimson, scale-plated centipede.

"Hey look, Trace, he's one of those bugs from the Third Circle." Sol stepped on the flailing lower carapace, pinning it. "Your favourite."

Grimacing as the thick fluid seeped around her boots, she said, "Ugh, nothing needs that many legs. Please squish it."

Sol shifted his weight and heard a crack. Smiled. Pulled the blade out, flipping the demon around. The illusion reasserted itself and Flea pulled himself up until he was sitting with his back to the car door. "Should I squish you Flea? Or are you going to open the god damn portal."

Flea's tanned skin, natty attire, and feathered hair took on a distinctly frayed aspect. The demon coughed black ooze. "I…" he wheezed, "can't. Even if… I wanted to."

The blade flashed and the fiend lost an arm, or half a dozen as the case may be, scaled appendages splashing into the still expanding puddle.

"I don't think you understand the gravity of the situation Flea. This knife can kill you. Like permanently. You'll regrow those limbs I'm sure, but you won't regrow your head. Now, I'm only going to ask once more before I end you, and Trace wastes time summoning one of your peers."

"You don't… fucking listen, do… you freaks? I said I couldn't. I… they took away our portal keys."

"Shit." Sol glanced at Trace. If that was actually true, then summoning another wasn't going to help.

Trace took the dagger from his hand and stood over Flea. "You know what Flea, I actually believe you. But, you forgot one thing. How did *you* get here?"

Flea's eyes darted to his car.

"Of course," she said, jamming the dagger into his forehead and snapping her fingers.

The blade and demon disintegrated into ash, catching the breeze and floating away.

"What the hell was that?" he asked.

"What was what?"

Sol snapped his fingers. Or tried to, his sweaty fingers producing more of a wet pop.

She shook her head as she cracked open the SUV's door. "You really gotta get out more."

Picking up his bag and trotting around to the passenger side, he slapped his hand on the hood. "Now I remember, it's a poetry thing, right?"

"No. Yes. You know what? Let's just pretend it was and stop talking about it before I get riled up."

"I like you riled up, it makes you hot and horny and sexy. You hate poets, though, and musicians."

"Hate's a strong word." Trace leaned over and grabbed his hair, planting a hard kiss after he climbed in and pushed his seat back. "I don't hate them all, just one or three. Or seven. And it doesn't matter anymore, does it?"

They both looked out their respective windows.

"You ever miss them?"

"Why are we even talking about this?" Trace snarled, starting the SUV. It roared to life, Spotify blasting "She's Kerosene" from a dozen speakers. She put the hammer down and accelerated, drifting around the circle, the world outside inverting like an x-ray negative before resolving to a harsh deep red.

Sol opened his window and leaned out, instantly sweating when the hot sulphurous air billowed in. Cranked up the A/C. "Hasn't changed a bit."

Chunky desert stretched endlessly in three directions. In the fourth, to their left, rose two massive gates of adamant, framed in black obsidian. Surrounding the gate, in a set of concentric arcs, sprawled an expanse of colourful tents and stone buildings through which snaked a line of hunched figures, shuffling forward, in lockstep.

The Bazaar, where the doomed had one final chance to make a deal with the worst sorts of fiends, and where just about anything could be bought or sold if you had the right currency.

"Can I see the list again?"

She tossed it to him and eased the SUV over the rise and down a long escarpment, brimstone crunching under the wheels.

"Most of these look pretty straightforward, but I'm not sure about a couple. Night Blooming Tulip? What the fuck is that? And the last one..." Sol scratched his crotch.

"It's a fucking freebee is what that is, no matter what Flea said."

"Does seem simple."

"Very. So, where to first?"

"I bet we can knock off a couple of easy ones at Sathariel's. Let's head there."

"Sure." She floored it, tearing up the ground until they reached a trio of Eucalyptus green tents the near edge of the city.

A bikini clad woman in lotus pose on a chaise lounge looked up as they parked. Squinting over the top of her Ray Bans, a smile leapt to her face and disappeared just as quickly.

"Still smoking hot, I see," said Sol, grabbing the straps of his duffle and resting his hand on the door handle.

"Think she's glad to see us? You know, after last time."

"No. But business is business."

"Let me do the talking."

He opened the door and hauled himself out, knees crackling.

"Nice ride," said the woman, with a throaty purr. "A giant step up from that shit box motorhome. Win the lottery or something?"

"Or something," said Trace, padding across the shattered brimstone and under the awning. She leaned down and gave the woman a lingering kiss.

"Mmmm, nice." The woman's smile returned, sharp teeth against blood red lips. She looked over at Sol, still leaning on the car door. Tipped her head. "Solomon."

"Sathariel."

"He's a wicked one, Trace, a hard soul, like Michael Madsen before he got pasty and fat. I'm glad you kept him."

"Me too."

"You know you're not supposed to be here, right? Always messing around where you shouldn't and turning up like bad pennies. I have half a mind to feed both of you to Gha'agsheblah for all the trouble you've caused me."

"Just following my nature." Trace ran a finger down the fallen angel's arm, shuddering when Sathariel grabbed her wrist and kissed the inside of it.

Sol cleared his throat and tilted his head towards the Bazaar.

"Right," said Trace, tugging away and fishing out the list. "We're here on business."

"Of course you are," said Sathariel, fanning herself with an elegant hand.

"For now." Trace tapped the list. "We need a few things."

"Let me see that."

Trace handed it over and settled back, arms crossed.

"A soul-bound Factory contract?" Sathariel shot both of them a stern look. "Fucking idiots. There's always one item that —"

Trace cut her off. "Yeah, yeah, we know what we're into. Now, got any of that stuff?"

Sathariel pulled Trace onto her lap and shouted into the tent. "Tham-tham, get out here, right now."

A red-black imp, mostly head and bulging eyes, scurried out, blinking in the harsh light.

"We have any Hellhound piss? Powdered adamant?"

The imp looked at her, looked at Trace and Sol. Licked his fat lips. "If it isn't Mr. and Mrs. Black. I heard you were dead. Or something. We talking cash or trade?" The voice of a ten pack-a-day smoker assaulted Sol's ears, the bass so low it made his chest hurt.

"Trade," said Sol. He slid the duffle onto the car's hood. Pulled out a black cloth bundle and rolled it open.

With a jump, the imp was on the front bumper, clambering up the grill with long clawed fingers. He picked at the revealed objects and selected a small green box sealed with a Thelemic unicursal hexagram. "Cards?"

"A tarot deck. Once belonged to Aleister Crowley."

"And the rest?"

"Teeth from a Saint, freshly dug up. Cherubim blood, shard of red brass from a Djinn lamp, and a

Book of the Dead. One of the old, real ones, not a cheap copy."

"The blood is fake, Cherubim is Dark Venetian Red, this," the imp held it up, let the orange glow soak through it. "This is English Vermilion. Dead giveaway."

Sol cursed under his breath.

"What Saint?" asked the imp.

"Does it matter?"

Tham-Tham leaned towards him, fishy breath filling the air. Rubbed his fingers together. "Immensely."

"Nicholas Charnetsky."

"Blessed Nicholas Charnetsky?" He laughed and the car vibrated. "Trying to pass off a Blessed as a real Saint is dangerous. And worthless. Well, to Sathariel at least. Some of the other... less discriminating proprietors might show interest."

"Yeah, I'll keep that in mind," said Sol, frowning to himself.

"We have other stuff," said Trace. She pulled out a battered pack of Slims, slipped the elastic off and opened the top. Showed the contents to the imp.

"Musician fingers, nice. Penises are the hot item right now, but there's always a market for bits of murdered musicians. And poets. Tempting, very tempting."

Sol snagged the cigarette package from her hand. "I can't believe you kept those."

"Waste not, isn't that what you always say?"

"Intimate with the original owner?" asked the imp.

"Could say that." She punched Sol's shoulder as he glowered. "I couldn't bear to listen to them thrum that fucking guitar any more. I did the world a favour, trust me."

"Not going to argue with that," said Sol. "Now, imp, what the hell do you want?"

"The car." Tham-tham pushed his face against the windshield and peered inside. "It's perfect. Exactly what we need."

"Trace?"

She shrugged. "There's other ways to get home and I'd just drive it off a cliff. Plus, I despise white. So..." she rubbed the red ribbon around her neck, "unspoiled."

Sathariel nibbled the back of Trace's neck. "We don't need a car either, Tham-tham. We've been over this, your feet can't reach the pedals."

"There's that messed up French guy that hangs around the cantina, claims he used to be a chauffeur of sorts."

"We don't need a car. Idiot. Take the... I don't know, the red brass and the cards."

"But..."

"NO." The air boomed and everyone jumped.

"But," he squeaked. "It's Mephistopheles's. I can smell it. Can't you? The shoeshine and hair spray? Besides," he looked at Trace and Solomon and flashed his teeth, "I know someone who'll pay plenty."

"HA!!" Her laugh was a second blast of thunder. She ran her hand through Trace's hair and smiled at Sol. "Flea's? You two always did surprise me. It's a deal."

The imp clapped his claws, hopped off the hood, and scurried into the tent, returning a moment later with a vial filled with bright yellow liquid and a small leather bag tied with a black drawstring.

Trace pried herself off Sathariel. "Later. I'll be back later, I promise."

Sathariel purred, leaning back and straightening her sunglasses.

"If we have time, baby. Let's get going, we have work to do." Sol started walking down a side road flanked by unoccupied tents, stopping to wait while the two she-devils said goodbye. Trace skipped over and slapped his ass.

"Two down, six to go," she said. "I have a good feeling about this."

"You always have a good feeling about everything." He watched her twirl, head back and arms out, laughing. "I'm thinking we should hit The Constantine next, see if Eleazar is still around. If anyone knows where to find a corrupted Notarikon, it's him. Plus he'll want that Book of the Dead—"

Pop. Pop. Pop.

Sol's leg burned and he shoved Trace hard, knocking her to the roadway, dropping on top of her. His Mossberg boomed into the darkened maw of a small pavilion to their left, and he heard the *crack* of Trace firing into the same patch of shadow. Metal clattered on crushed brimstone followed by a heavy thump and a gurgle.

"You're bleeding," said Trace, nudging him off, gun trained on the opening.

The gurgle slowed to a stop. "I think we got the shooter."

"Quit changing the subject. How bad is it? Truth."

He forced out a little cough-laugh. "Non-fatal."

"Hmmf." She wormed forward to disappear into the gloom.

Keeping her covered, eyes scanning the surrounding structures, he poked at the bloody patch on his thigh. Winced. Maybe he was getting old, getting clipped like that. They knew better than to go traipsing around like they owned the place. Well, *he* did anyways.

Crack.

"Clear," she called, striding back and helping him to his feet and into a secluded alcove, digging the first aid kit out of his duffle. She kissed his chest, undid his belt, and yanked down his pants, clicking her tongue as she cleaned out the shallow gash. When she finished, she pressed a couple of painkillers into his hand. "You're not going to like it."

"Barely feel it, thanks." He kissed her forehead.

"I mean the shooter."

"Not a scavenger?"

"Adrienne." She started along the roadway, gun in hand.

"Shit." He choked down the pills and hurried after her, leg already stiffening up. "You sent her to Hell the hard way."

"And guess where she turned up?"

"I mean Hell-Hell, there's no way she got out of line. What did she have to sell? One of her god-awful free verse chapbooks?"

"If she wriggled out of it who knows who else might be lurking around. I'm glad you packed extra shells, 'cause I plan on double-murdering anyone that looks at us funny."

Keeping a sharp eye out, they paid a visit to The Constantine, a used bookstore of sorts, overflowing with the written word. Eleazar hadn't changed, still the bookish old Jewish grandfather everyone wished they had. As Sol figured, he exchanged the Book of the Dead for an amulet inscribed with a Notarikon satanic bible verse.

"Oooh, do you see what I see?" said Trace, pulling Sol into the mouth of an alley between weathered stone buildings.

"A fabulous place for an ambush?"

"No, silly." She pointed at the green glow. "Starbucks!"

He almost laughed. Why wouldn't there be a Starbucks? They padded down the alley, passing an unmarked red door as the shadows deepened and the alley's denizens grew more distinct: classic crimson horned devils and slug like monstrosities, all eyes and mouths and slime. The demons sat, leaned, and draped, filling a long, narrow patio with chittering and buzzing, pouring overpriced coffee down assorted gullets.

The café itself was a shining gem in an ancient, pitted setting. Bright. Clean. Modern. Except the sign. The mermaid blazed in its original bare breasted glory. The lone barista, pink haired and perfect, beamed at them when they reached the counter.

"What can I get you," she said, her voice angelic.

Standing on her toes, Trace squinted at the drink list. "Jackpot!" She clutched at Sol and bounced. "Night Blooming Tulip Tea."

"New," said the barista. "Well, newish. Only place you can get it. Unless," and she pointed a tattooed arm towards the ground, "you are totally fucked."

"Don't you know it, sister," said Trace. "Now, while the tea does sound interesting, I'm in need of something with a little more kick. Can I get a Venti Hellfire Roast? With room."

"Of course." Brilliant white teeth flashed and she turned to Sol. "And for you?"

"I'm good."

"Indeed." She looked back at Trace. "Anything else?"

"Yeah, we need some Night Blooming Tulip... not the tea, but like, the actual stuff."

"We do sell the concentrate, but it is an import item and quite expensive."

"Ring a bottle up. What currency do you take?"

The angel glanced around, eyes half closing. "A variety. The locals, most of them anyways, pay with well... information about the goings on in these parts. But you, being tourists, are a different story." She reached out, brushing Trace's red ribbon.

Trace inched back and put a hand to her throat. "No, I'd die first."

"I understand. There's power there. Memory bound up. Blood. Murder. Forbidden love. The Boss desires tokens like that." She tapped the counter. "I guess I'll have to request something a little more... intimate."

Trace's eyes narrowed. "What, like my panties? What kind of angel are you?"

The smile again. "I'll settle for your heart."

"Don't even think about it," growled Sol, grabbing her arm and pulling harder than he should have.

She jerked away, slipping her purse off a shoulder. "Relax, I got this."

"Like hell you do. No deals like that here. Ever. It was bad enough taking that fucking contract." He loomed over her, glared at the barista who kept on smiling. "Besides, I'm a fifty percent owner and I'm not selling."

Trace tilted her head back, "You're such a romantic. One of the reasons I love you so much. But it's not what you think." She dug around in her bag, pulled out fist-sized jar of Merlot coloured liquid, and placed it on the counter.

The barista touched it, tracing a porcelain finger around the rim. "Perfect."

"What the flying fuck?" Sol watched her snatch it up and vanish into the back room. "Whose heart was that?"

"You don't want to know," said Trace, snuggling against his chest. "So, don't ask."

"But—"

She touched a finger to his lips. "Please."

The magic word. He took a deep breath and slid the tip of his finger between her throat and Choncey's ribbon.

"It's an old ribbon Sol, and like she said, full of memory. But I love it. It reminds me of those crazy times, and I never want to forget any of them."

"Still…"

"And you worry waaaay too much. What's done is done, and while those were glorious days, these are better." She gave him a huge squeeze.

A polite cough broke the spell. "Here you are, enjoy," said the barista, placing a coffee and small apothecary bottle of black fluid on the edge of the counter. "And," she gave a final picture-perfect smile, "come back soon."

"Thanks," said Trace, snagging the steaming coffee and carrying it to the milk station. She dropped it hard and blew on her hand. "Holy crap that's hot."

Sol held up the bottle. Not black, as he first thought, but a deep red. He examined the label. "Night Blooming Tulip. For commercial alchemical use only. If consumed orally, side effects may include nausea, visions, insatiable lust, and/or death." He'd heard of it, of course, one of those rare occult ingredients desired by fringe artists. What the hell would the Factory want with it? Nothing noble, of that he was certain. He watched Trace top her coffee off with cream, snag a lid, and slide on three cardboard heat sleeves.

"Damn it," she said, taking a tiny sip and many quick breaths. "They didn't skimp on the hellfire. So, big guy, where next?"

"We're half done and like you said, the last one is easy. Let's hit the Emporium, it's a rat hole full of junk, but there's a good chance they'll have the rest of this stuff."

They exited the alley at its busy end, where it intersected a radial spoke road leading to the great gates.

"Left or right?" asked Trace, glancing back over her shoulder as they stepped out onto the roadway.

Sol heard an engine roar and grabbed the back of her dress, yanking her back as a dusty white Porsche swerved right at them. In the split second before the side mirror caught his shoulder, he caught a glimpse of the occupants behind the heavy tinting: the driver's head tilted at an impossible angle atop crooked, stooped shoulders, and the passenger's Bride of Frankenstein hair bent back against the sunroof.

Crack, crack, crack. Trace unleashed a torrent of bullets, blowing out the back windows of the SUV and punching holes everywhere else. The Porsche fishtailed, but the driver kept control like a pro and surged away, smashing through a number of lunch kiosks and shrieking demonic vendors before disappearing down a side road a few hundred yards away.

"You dead?" asked Trace, jamming a fresh magazine into her Herstal.

"Mostly," groaned Sol. He rolled over onto his back and stared up at the orange, flickering sky.

Trace spat out a mouthful of dust. "That fucking imp. Once we're done I'm going to find him and cut him into very tiny pieces."

It hadn't been the imp. No. The hair was unmistakeable. Cindy Lou. Partner in Crime. Friend. Lover. One point on the pentagram that burned so bright before exploding so spectacularly. He'd seen her, alive and well, only last summer.

And the driver. Sol knew those shoulders; he'd sat beside them in the Chief for two years, watching the blacktop of America roll by.

Those people. This place. A terrible suspicion crept into his mind. She wouldn't have…

"I'm beginning to remember what I hated most about this blasted dump," said Trace, crawling over to him. "Everyone's a fucking asshole." She pulled up the sleeve of his shirt and poked and prodded, prompting a coarse grunt. "Not broken, but you're going to have one hell of a bruise. Take more aspirin and call me in the morning."

Sol rubbed his shoulder, trying not to meet her eyes. "I need a drink."

"That," she said, digging around in her bag yet again, "is a prescription I can fill." She handed him a thin, silver flask.

He unscrewed the cap and took a searing pull of bourbon. "I love you."

"I love you too. Now pull yourself together. We've overstayed our welcome."

Sol dragged himself to his feet, mind churning. He should ask. He should. But her look, her tone, at Starbucks. *Please.* Trust was a terrible thing.

They went right, winding their way through a maze of side streets and alleys choked with the opportunistic barrel scrapings of demonkind and reeking of flesh and rotten eggs. The great gates loomed higher, wider, and he caught glimpses of the ragged, doomed horde marching down the main boulevard. He knew what awaited them on the other side. Suffering. Not forever, of course. Nothing was forever. But the wicked paid, each according to their sins.

The Emporium itself was a flea market like no other in existence. While most traders in the Bazaar dealt in the exotic, the Emporium specialized in the dregs gleaned from the worst and poorest of the processional. An ocean of junk, but oh, what junk.

Want a baby pacifier from a crib death? An obol folks figure will get them across the River Styx until they realize Hellenic Hell got acquired during the 9th Century Underworld Consolidation Wars? A rich man's needle, complete with camel fur? Each had intrinsic value to their original owner, but most were curiosities. Hellbound junk.

"How the fuck are we going find shit in this mess?" Trace asked, wrinkling her nose.

"Ah," said Sol, "that's the beauty of this disaster. You just need to ask." He approached a tall, spindly collection of pitted iron legs heaped against a nearby tent pole. A demon mantis unfolded itself and dropped into a crouch, thorax buzzing. Sol nodded and snagged the list, pointing to the three items.

Another buzz.

Trace scratched behind her ear with the barrel of her pistol. "What's it saying?"

"That we're idiots for taking a Factory contract, but the items shouldn't be a problem. It's just a matter of cost."

Sol pulled the cloth roll from his bag and rolled it on the floor. The demon prodded the displayed treasures with a wire-bristled foreleg and buzzed again, the intonation unmistakable.

"Fuck."

"What?"

"He wants something more modern, more technological, more… um, hip. I swear it's another goddamn Millennial."

"Give me a sec." Trace sat, balancing the Herstal on a knee, and rummaged through her purse. Found a bundle of iTunes gift cards wrapped in elastic and tossed it at him.

"You steal anything else last night?"

"Of course."

"Why do I bother to ask?" Sol waved the bundle and the bug buzzed, purring like the happiest, rustiest cat in the universe. A foreleg reached out, the hairs accepting the cards like a sacred offering. In a blink the demon scuttled into the vendor jungle.

"That was surprisingly easy," said Trace, standing up and stretching. "You sure it's coming back?"

"No."

"Right then." She handed him her flask. "I thought this'd be way harder."

"Well," Sol said once the bug returned from its successful hunt and they'd located the closest human compatible bar, "that just leaves the last... item. Emissions Nocturnal." He rubbed his bruised shoulder and leaned back on the distressed leather wrapped wood of the booth seat. Took a sip from his drink and checked his watch. "It's technically night."

Trace pulled a short, wide mouthed Mason jar from her bag and spun it across the table. "Gotcha covered, old man." She disappeared under the table.

He felt her hands slide over his crotch, fingers tracing the seams of his pants. Felt her undo his belt, pop the button, tug down his zipper. Taking a deep breath, he closed his eyes and tangled a hand in her hair. "You're a beast."

"Thanks, lover. Though you're not lacking in the beastly department either." Her disembodied voice seemed to come from nowhere and everywhere.

"Before you blow... my mind, I wrote you a poem."

A bump under the table. "What?"

"Well, not a good poem or anything. Want to hear it?"

"Hmm."

He felt her start and fumbled for the paper he'd jammed into his duffel hours before. Smoothed it out, propping it against the Mossberg.

"Golden mane, golden curls.

Catching the wind, rustling, impatient.

Writhing.

But there is no wind.

Just curls, coiling, uncoiling.

Twisted, hungry.

So hungry.

Always hungry.

For bones, and blood, and souls — "

A sharp bite cut him off.

"That's sweet," she said, giving him a moment's grace. "Don't write another."

"One time only, I promise." Though he wasn't sure about that.

Trace practiced her magic and his heart raced, blood pounding. The end was near. Sol reached out to grab his drink and terrible pain lanced through is forearm. Shit, let your guard down for one fucking minute and it all goes to hell. Literally. He opened his eyes and saw the knife pinning his arm to the tabletop, and with his other hand still ensnared in the hungry curls he'd just effused, he almost panicked. Almost. Instead he relaxed, considering his trump card, and sagged back against the bench cushions as a shadow blocked the dingy light and someone or something snatched the Mossberg away.

"Solomon." A low rasp.

Sol felt Trace stop short. He twisted and looked up at the ragged thing, stooped and crooked, head bent down and to the side. An angry red wound torn across its throat.

"Choncey."

"Hands... your other hand where I can see it if you would, old... friend."

Sol tugged and felt Trace extract his entangled fingers, giving them a gentle squeeze. He brought his hand out and placed it on the table, attempting to not jostle his other arm. It didn't hurt as much as it should and he was grateful the rotgut hell spirits were taking the edge off.

"Where's Trace, Solomon? I want what's mine. This isn't about you, so don't make it that way."

Choncey. So, it *had* been him driving the Porsche. And that meant it *had* been Cindy Lou in the passenger seat. He stared at the man's slit throat and stiffened. Trace shifted under the table, quiet. Secret. So many secrets.

"She's not here." The lie floated through his lips and he noticed their busted old driver wasn't alone. Two figures flanked him. A slender man, fingerless, guitar slung over his beat-up leather vest, and a woman with beehive hair sporting a gaping hole in her chest. The pentagram reunited. Behind them stood others, a veritable rogues gallery. Sol recognized most of them. Poets. Artists. Old friends. Old enemies.

Crack. Crack. Crack. Crack. Crack.

Choncey sprouted holes and reeled away with a wheeze. The vengeful dead scattered, tripping over each other in an effort to find cover through the spray of bullets. Sol tore the knife from his arm and drew the 1911, popping a couple of shots at the slowpokes before ducking and sliding down to join Trace. Return fire raked the table and bench.

Sol winced, struggling to pull his pants up, the booth exploding around them.

"No regrets," said Trace before he had a chance to say anything. She ejected her clip and jammed in another. Blood ran down a cheek caressed by slivers of hardwood.

What did he have to say, anyways? That she was a fucking psychopath who murdered everyone she ever loved? He jolted when a stray shell grazed his weeping arm and they locked eyes, ice green boring into slate grey. Between popping off rounds, he grabbed the back of her neck, fingers catching on her damn ribbon, a *gift* from Choncey so long ago, and gave her a hard kiss.

The smile made it all worth it.

Sol launched himself from under the disintegrating table, keeping low and firing at any hint of movement. He heard Trace unleash her own version of Hell behind him and he tripped when something slammed into his leg. He rolled and staggered up, drilling a poet once known as Rifflet Bob in the forehead, the back of the man's silver head splashing against the wall. The shadows deepened, oblivion seeping through the air and Sol stumbled towards the door leading outside, Trace still in his shadow. She said something about love and he reached, fingers snagging on her when a bullet hit his hip. Another smashed into his back, driving him forward and down, through the door and onto the street. He lost his grip on his gun, hearing it tumble away.

The x-ray inversion caught him by surprise this time, the sudden transition stealing his breath and the accompanying after-images searing his vision. Too soon, he screamed to himself. I can't go back. Not yet. He fumbled for his gun, without any luck, until his sight returned.

The street was deserted, the buildings, somewhat familiar, fallen to ruin. Great black gates, twins to the doorstep of hell, stood closed. Abandoned. Doom hung in the ozone-tinged air and immense shapes lumbered in the distance.

Realization dawned. Not home. Not Hell.

"Trace!" Ancient nothingness swallowed his voice.

Sol crawled to a block of shattered stone and leaned against it, not feeling his wounds, the pain. Anything.

"Trace?"

But there was no Trace.

She'd seen him fall and been right behind him. She'd follow. Wouldn't she?

Time passed. An eternity.

And he waited, fist tight around the scarlet ribbon, then letting it go.

Deep Pressure

Sarah L. Johnson

Rush hour on a downtown train. The home stretch. Passengers jostle, stirring up echoes of perfume under a rime of sweat. The smell is a prelude, a thick temptation. It rolls out the open doors onto the platform, and reels me in with a promise.

Deep pressure.

Bodies touching, crowding, crushing – and all of them trying not to. All but me. I want it, I need it, and I'll go crazy without it. I am the unstoppable force in constant search of the next immoveable object.

But tonight, the unstoppable force had to work late.

I don't like leaving the Factory after dark, but a contract came last minute, and I needed to deploy the team. Top notch client service means I missed rush hour. The cars are all but deserted as they clatter to a stop along the platform. I press the dirty green button. The door opens with a sigh that says it all.

Better luck tomorrow.

Fluorescent lights show every seat vacant. No one to crush. The only thing left is their scent, just enough to make my palms itch. In the glass that is window by day, mirror by night, I see the reflection of a woman: sensible skirt with sensible shoes, hair pulled back. Normal. But inside the need grows, contained by a taut membrane about to burst. Perhaps if I pack myself tightly into a corner, hang on until...

I see you.

Lying on a bench at the elbow of the car. A few steps closer and I'm standing on the circular pivot in the floor, standing over an opportunity. I rub my fingertips together, thinking.

You're out cold, sprawled on your stomach. Your green mohawk crunches against the back of the seat and your face droops with steel piercings. Sleeves of tattoos disappear into a Stiff Little Fingers t-shirt. Ink scrolls up your neck to jacket your shaved scalp. Fierce armor. But underneath, old wounds. A born victim.

A flush unfurls across my chest.

I've never done more than crush, never more than press my ache against an unwitting lover through layers of nylon and wool. No skin, no groping – just deep pressure. I'm a thief. A vampire, siphoning off what I need, something my lover will never miss. They never know.

Later, in the dark, I'll slip between two thick mattresses. Memory foam, for remembering. I'll finish in private, what I began in public. Hand between my legs, writhing against the weight conforming to every inch of my body.

I've never done more.

But here you are. I kneel to get a closer look. Your eyeliner is smudged, though I can tell you applied it with care. You smell like a chemical fire. I shake your shoulder. Nonreactive. Drugs? Overdose? I should punch that red emergency button. You might be slipping into a coma. But you're breathing well enough, at least for now. It's my breath that comes in low, greedy gulps. There's a reason people like me are called mouth-breathers.

I'll just stay here and keep an eye. I'll take care of you. We'll take care of each other. The train rumbles around a sharp bend and I shift with the circle in the floor – curving away and back again. Can you feel what I need from you? That would ruin everything. The critical ingredient in my pathology is the very thing that defines it as pathological.

I want to pull you off the bench, drape your body over mine and let you flatten me into the gritty, stamped-rubber floor. But that would be difficult to explain, should someone board the car. So I sit on the bench, slide my hands under your shoulders, lift, scoot over and slowly – so slowly – lower your head to rest on my lap.

Oh...

You're heavy on my thighs, pressing me into the padded bench. Wet heat builds as I imagine all of me, beneath all of you. How would it feel to wrap my legs around you, while your weight forces the air from my lungs.

My legs part. I reach under my skirt. Your breath mists across my inner thigh. Green hair abrades the inside of my wrist, burning like a criminal's brand as I stroke myself.

A lock of hair falls over my forehead, brown and dull, washed out – like the rest of me. But you. Everything about you breathes color. If I cut you, the sunset would run from your veins. Or perhaps you'd bleed ink. Your tattoos, variegated swirls of black, red and blue, pulse vivid and alive against my beige skirt. What are they? One tattoo, expanded upon? Or many, braided together? A dragon on the wing, slicing into an ocean wave, spiraling upward in a cyclone of flame and teeth, possibly covering a name. Someone who broke your heart.

I will never hurt you.

The train lurches. Your hand flails and lands with a slap on my wrist. I skim my short nails over your skull and neck, soothing you back into deeper unconsciousness. But the mild sting from your palm releases a flood of toxic arousal and I need more pressure.

I slip off my shoes and wedge one leg under your torso. Denim, brass rivets, and a wallet chain imprint on my flesh. Your head rests in the cradle between my hipbones. Can you hear the whoosh of blood through my aorta? I thrust my pelvis, testing the weight. Then I take your hand in mine. Soft skin, silver rings, and nails just grimy enough to give me pause.

Escalation.

But the warning passes with the heat of your face against my belly. Faint murmuring, rapid eye movement. To think I've been making do with an arm pressed to mine, my breasts politely squashed against the back of a stranger.

Your eyelids shudder. Are you dreaming of me? If you were to wake up, what would you do? Would you be angry? Would you cry?

I peel my panties aside and manipulate your hand until those dirty nails and tarnished silver slide along the slippery furnace of my cunt. The train shimmies and squeals. Your forked tongue lolls between parted lips. A deliberate surgical body mod. Saliva soaks through my blouse like acid through an eggshell and I imagine your two-pronged tongue flicking against my thighs.

"I love you."

The words fall on deaf ears but I mean them from the bottom of my heart. The train howls through a tunnel. I force your fingers inside me. Wedged beneath you, my left foot cries with pins and needles. I clench hard around the invasion of your hand. Pressure from without, from within. Deep. Your fingers twitch and I rupture, drowning in my own sickness.

For several minutes I lay there, deflated. When I finally gaze down at your face, your lips are purple, edging into blue. You aren't breathing nearly so well now. Sore and empty, I squirm out from under you. Once more I stand on the circular pivot, curving away and back again. A ding announces the upcoming station. It isn't my stop but think I should get off now.

Our lips meet and I lick the sour crotch of your tongue. Then I kiss your ear, whispering, "I'm sorry."

The doors open with a gasp. You really don't look well, and I promised I'd take care of you. Before I step onto the platform, I smack my palm against the big red button.

8-Ball

Robert Bose

Billy shook the black plastic sphere for the umpteenth time, glaring when the prophetic triangle remained dark.

"Rachel!" he screamed up the stairs. "This piece of shit is busted."

"What?" His older sister's voice rose above the heavy metal din.

"I said your fucking 8-Ball is fucked."

"What?"

"It's fucking FUCKED!"

The hardwood thumped as Rachel emerged from her room, scowling over the railing, eyes peering from under choppy platinum hair. "What the hell are you going on about?"

"Your magic 8-Ball."

"Jesus, where'd you find that that thing?"

"In your panty drawer."

"Right," she said, spinning and marching out of sight.

Billy raced up the stairs and pounded on the closing door. "Rach! I'm sorry, just a joke. It was under your bed."

The door flew open and her hand caught the front of his shirt, yanking him close until their foreheads touched. "You're digging that hole deeper, asshole. When were you in my room?"

"Last night, when you were at the bar."

His sister let him go, eyes narrowing at him, at the 8-Ball. "Shit, that one's like a bad penny."

"This one? There's more?"

"Yeah, I pulled two out of the Factory crate we found behind Arby's. Tossed 'em both in a dumpster weeks ago."

"It still has real magic in it, right?"

"Where did you say you found it?"

"Under your bed, way at the back, behind all your notebooks full of… poetry."

Her face flushed. "What's your damn problem anyways? Girl trouble again?"

He shrugged and jammed the Magic 8-Ball into her face. "It's busted. Needs new arcane new batteries or something."

She snatched it away, mumbled something, and rotated the sphere. The blue triangle shimmered and words appeared.

OUTLOOK NOT SO GOOD

"Let me see that." A shake and a flip and the screen flickered before fading to black. "Fuck. See?"

"Moron, you have to ask it a specific question. Out loud. And don't let it railroad you into anything. Trust me, it's not worth it."

What the hell did that mean? He sat on the stairs, feeling the floor vibrate when she cranked her music back up. A question. Alright. He held the 8-Ball tight and spoke, clearly and carefully. "Will Grace Turner sleep with me?" Turned it over.

ASK AGAIN LATER

Really? For fuck's sake. He'd been so close right before Christmas, gotten a hand up her shirt, but Tanner had caught her fancy and she'd all but forgotten how perfect they were for each other. And he had too, or so he'd thought. Until yesterday. Walking across the school parking lot – their eyes met – and now she consumed his thoughts, stoking old flames from cold crumbling embers.

He hefted the ball, thought about shattering it against the wall. Saw it shimmer again.

MIDNIGHT

Moonlight streamed through his bedroom window as Billy flicked through pictures of Grace on his phone: her gaping shirt revealing a push-up bra, the edge of her butt-cheeks peeking out from her cut-offs, a juicy upskirt. He almost felt bad about taking that one. Almost.

11:56 p.m.

He stared at the upskirt, zooming in until the crooked flash of black lace was a blurry sea of grey. The lack of resolution infuriated him. Hadn't he waited long enough? He wanted her. He needed her. And she needed him too.

As the final minutes ticked by, clouds obscured the moon and a cool breeze rustled the blinds, bringing with it a hint of rain. Billy burrowed under his blankets and rubbed the black ball like a rosary, giving it a little shake the moment his alarm clock flipped from 11:59 to 12:00.

"I want Grace Turner. Will I get her?"

A blue glow infused the room.

TOMORROW

He hugged the ball to his chest. His sister was right, there was magic in this old relic.

The triangular screen morphed from blue to scarlet.

THE FIRST ONE IS FREE

Self-confidence was currency at Blessed Nicholas Charnetsky High School and Billy spent liberally the next morning, buying smiles and nods as he bounced through the halls, on top of the world after a dreary January.

A hand slapped his back when he opened his locker and tossed his bag inside.

"Get your dick caught in the vacuum again, Willy?" Pecker Paul leaned on the next door, tugging at the patchy scrub he called a beard.

"Ha, you know what?" Billy said, grinning. "I'm not even going tell you how ugly your ugly face is today. I'm better than that."

"So, seriously, what's up?"

"Well, nothing… yet. But the good times are here." Billy grabbed his crotch. "If you get my drift."

"Who?"

"Who do you think?"

"Not going to happen, Willy my boy. You're beating a dead unicorn."

"Shush." Billy held up a hand, eyes on the chestnut-haired girl floating down the hallway. She was short and a little chubby, with a crooked smile and great tits, both glowing in the fluorescent light.

"Hi Grace," he called out.

She stopped, hazel eyes smoldering. "Billy, I was just thinking about you."

Pecker cleared his throat. "Well, I gotta go, nice seeing you Grace."

Her hand snagged Pecker's arm. "Grats on making the Basketball team, Paul. Sounds like the Saints might have a chance this year after all. I'll come cheer you on."

"Uh, thanks." The lanky boy pushed off the locker and rambled down the hall, looking back over his shoulder.

"I've been thinking about you too," said Billy, leaning in, compressing their personal space and inhaling her piquant scent. His brain and body caught fire. Memories of his hand tracing from her belly button up to her rib cage burned across his mind. "Do you... you know... want to get together? Hang out? Maybe continue where we, uh, left off?"

Grace shifted, twisting, but not widening the gap. "Uh..."

The flames intensified. "I... You said you were thinking of me. I just need — "

"Look, I like you Billy. More than I should. But I have a boyfriend right now and that wouldn't... you know. I was thinking about you because I'm looking for *The Hellbound Heart*. You mentioned you had one and I'd love to borrow it."

"Oh." He shrunk in on himself, the flames dwindling.

"But don't give up," she said, walking away with a glint in her eye. "I won't have a boyfriend forever."

That night in his room, Billy flopped on his back and shook the 8-Ball violently.

"Why?" He knew it wasn't a proper question, but he didn't give a flying fuck.

Vibrant blue seared his retinas.

BECAUSE

"Because what?" He knew this was crazy, taking advice and who knows what else from a piece of rotten plastic, but it didn't matter.

YOU MUST PAY

He thought about Grace, the line of her cleavage. Her lips. That crooked, inviting smile. The way she'd flip her hair when she was annoyed or excited. And she'd talked to him today, even if he hadn't gotten everything he'd wanted. The words rang in his head. The first one is free. The first one. He took a deep, hot breath, sweat dripping from his face and arms.

"Tell me the price."

The screen began to fade and he cursed, realizing his mistake.

"What... what is the price?"

TERRACE VII: WALL OF FIRE

The triangle blazed scarlet.

BLOOD

His opportunity arrived during gym class. With the regular teacher away, the sub let them loose in the gym, directing the boys to play dodge ball while he chatted up the girls. A creep, but who wouldn't do the same if given the opportunity?

Billy snapped a ball out of the air and scanned the scurrying rats for an appropriate victim. One boy stood out. Tanner. The boyfriend. Perfect. When his nemesis dove under a wicked curve and slide by, Billy let loose at point blank range, rubber meeting nose in spectacular fashion.

Tanner screamed.

The game stopped.

"No headshots Billy, what the hell is wrong with you?" barked one of the bossy jocks as he rushed over to Tanner with a towel.

Billy shrugged. "Sorry."

Pecker wandered over. "Harsh man. Very harsh."

"He changed directions at the last second. What can I say?"

"Still, bad karma."

Pecker joined the group helping the writhing, sputtering Tanner and Billy felt a hand brush his back, and a familiar scent, warm and spicy. Bad karma? Bullshit.

"Nice throw," said Grace.

Billy sent silent gratitude to the old 8-Ball. "I thought you were going out, what's up with that?"

She swayed, bumping her hip into his. "Nothing, not your problem, though you were the solution. You bring the book?"

"In my locker."

"Want to meet up at the Starbucks after last class? I have to deal with something first, so I may be late."

"Need any help?"

Grace patted his shoulder, sending a tingle into his groin. "You'll know if I do, trust me."

She didn't show up.

Billy waited at the school Starbucks, hoping for at least a text. He wanted to message her, but the direct approach hadn't worked last time and he knew, with an uncomfortable tightness spreading through his chest, that it wouldn't work this time.

The pink-haired barista started sweeping up, pausing when she got to his table.

"We're closing in ten minutes, William. Need anything else?"

"No, thanks." She was gorgeous and it honestly hurt to look right at her, so he stared at his phone and sipped his Refresher.

"Lust is a dangerous game, isn't it?"

He forced his gaze up, drawn into her sharp eyes. Didn't have a clue how to reply, so he kept his mouth shut for once.

"It seems so right, but burning desire is an infection, a curse. Don't let it railroad you into anything. Trust me, it's not worth it." Her words followed her back behind the counter.

Fuck that, even if she was right, it didn't matter. He sucked back the last of his lemonade and drove home, ignoring his parent's greetings, and stomped to his room where the 8-Ball winked from the nightstand. Fuck that too.

He ached. Inside. All over. A monstrous hand gripped his heart and squeezed: harder and harder and harder. Why did this have to be so goddamn painful? He liked her. Maybe even loved her. He had, from the first day of high school. Crooked, that's how he always thought of her. Crooked hair, a crooked smile, always looking half through you, as if you weren't quite there, but still making you feel special.

A knock on his door and Rachel's head poked in, brave considering the typical evening activities of a sex-starved seventeen-year-old boy, but his sister had few fears.

"You okay, bro?"

"Sure."

"Right..." Rachel padded in, and dropped a plate of food on his paper-strewn desk. "Dad barbequed foot-longs, thought you might be hungry." She sat down, leaning her arms on the back of his desk chair. "Want to talk about it?"

"No." He twisted his head, stared at the pinups dominating the wall, the long row of horror books packed onto shelves.

"I warned you."

They sat in silence, listening to the old house creak in the wind.

"What... what did you ask for?" he asked when it was obvious she wasn't going to leave.

"You wouldn't believe me."

"Maybe not last week, but now... what was it?"

"Doesn't matter. I may not be all that together, as this family never hesitates to remind me. But at least I know where to draw the line."

"Didn't work out then, did it?"

"No."

"How come?"

"The price, bro... Too steep, even for me." A tear ran down her cheek and she walked to the door, stopped as if she was going to say something else, but just closed it behind her.

The sun dipped below the horizon and the room dimmed. Grace was worth the price. Any price. Wasn't she?

"What's the price?" he whispered to the 8-Ball.

Another word, framed in scarlet.

BONE

His phone buzzed and he realized he hadn't let go of it the entire time he'd been home.

"The magic stairwell. Tomorrow. Noon."

He almost sent her a reply. Almost.

There was no magic in the stairwell, just stale weed smoke and the legendary reputation of a place where shit went down, locked and off-limits, while the school tried, to no avail, to clean up the toxic mould growing in the walls. They couldn't keep the determined out, of course, with security cameras and barriers vanishing after installation. The staff had largely given up – if idiot kids wanted to poison themselves for privacy, so be it.

Billy didn't make a habit of hanging out there. He didn't smoke and he didn't have a girlfriend to fondle in the dark. Still, he knew at least two ways to get in, Pecker being a useful source of uncommon common knowledge. He used the easiest way, through the air vent that crossed across the top of the boy's second floor bathroom.

When he pushed aside the vent cover and wiggled out into the dimly lit landing, he knew the smell was wrong, Drakkar Noir crowding out the tang of weed and mould. He crouched, letting his eyes adjust, and in the corner, where the stairs turned, someone leaned against the railing.

"Glad you could make it, Billy." Tanner walked up the stairs, nose swathed in bandages, flipping a bat onto his shoulder.

Shit, shit, shit. Billy knew he wouldn't get far without anywhere to run.

"You pasted me on purpose."

Billy pressed himself against the wall, lifted his hands up. "Who told you?"

"Doesn't... matter." Tanner sniffed, his sinuses solid. Eyes sunken and bruised. He hefted the bat. "But now you have to pay the price."

The way he said it sent a jolt through Billy's heart. Grace. She told him. She sent him. But it didn't matter. A hook twisted, the barb cutting deep, opening a raw, flaming wound. Billy's hands curled into fists and he pushed off the wall, head down, launching himself before Tanner could get a solid swing. The bat thumped against Billy's back. He dug his shoulder into Tanner's stomach, doing his football coach proud, and drove the other boy back on his heels, right to edge of the stairs.

With a grunt, Billy jerked back, watching Tanner teeter and then tumble down the stairwell, bat clattering away into darkness, thumps ending in a thick thud. He hadn't meant to push that hard. Well, he had and he hadn't. He took another step and watched Tanner suck slow, raspy breaths, the bandages covering his nose awash with fresh blood.

A steep price. A fair price? Cool doubt smothered his burning conviction.

"Sor…" No, he wasn't sorry and he wasn't going to apologize. More steps. "Let's get you out of here. I'll take you to the hospital."

Tanner's eyes, reduced to black beads, glinted in defiance. "No." It came out a wet cough.

"I mean it. We can sort this out later."

"Fuck you." The boy rolled half over to a sitting position, hissing sharply as he shifted what had to be a broken arm to his lap. "Just go away. Leave me the fuck alone."

Threads of sympathy stretched but didn't break. Billy walked up the steps and wiggled through the vent, back into the bowels of the school.

Grace waited at his locker. She looked up from her phone as he strode down the hall through the press of students, head down, hands jammed in his pocket.

"You okay?" she asked.

"Not really."

Her hand touched his arm. "Sorry… It's complicated." She ran her fingers along his bicep, tracing the muscle. "Sometimes extreme problems require extreme solutions. Right?"

He wanted to pull away. But he couldn't.

Fingernails dug in, squeezed. She stood on her tippy toes and kissed his cheek, pulling back when his lips turned to brush hers.

The bell roared, snapping him out of her spell.

"What do you need—" His question cut off as she disappeared into the rushing mob, the hint of jasmine and pepper lingering.

"Hear the news?" asked Pecker, catching up with him on the way to class.

Billy swallowed hard, shrugged.

"Tanner is having a real bad week, fell down some stairs and broke his arm and his collarbone."

"Extreme."

"Yeah, close call. But it could have been a lot worse."

Late night drives were peaceful, the empty roads illuminated by streetlights and the waxing moon. No old folks dawdling in crosswalks. No ice cream trucks. No clueless kids on bikes. No cops. Billy sped, blowing through stop signs and red lights, determined to make record time to his destination. He tried to keep his mind on the driving, unsuccessfully, and checked his phone again to make sure the text wasn't his imagination.

The single word, stark and bold and urgent.

"HELP"

After lunch he'd slunk through the afternoon in a haze, the world slipping by without notice. He ate dinner with his family, picking absently at his food, mumbling replies to mundane questions, and later, laying in bed, held the 8-Ball in one hand and his phone in the other, wishing he could toss both out the window.

He didn't ask a question. Something held him back. Made him hesitate. He wasn't even sure what he *should* ask. How far could this go?

The text interrupted his contemplation.

"HELP"

His sister blocked the front door as he half hopped, half sprinted down the stairs, pulling up his pants and trying to fix his flattened hair all at the same time.

"Don't go, bro," she said. "I don't doubt you'll get what you want, but is it worth the price?"

"She's in trouble. She needs my help."

"That doesn't answer my question."

"I don't have a choice."

Without another word, Rachel surrendered the door.

"HELP"

Billy took the final turn onto Grace's street without slowing, still speeding when a figure limped out on the road in front of him. His foot touched the brake and the person pinned by his headlights turned, arm in a cast and face bandaged. Tanner. Tanner leaving Grace's house, shirt torn, face twisted in rage, good hand balled in a fist.

In a fraction of a second he knew the question, the answer, and the final price for his wish. He didn't have to do anything, just keep going. A terrible accident they'd say. A tragedy. He'd have paid in blood, in bone, in life. He'd get the girl.

But... he knew something else.

His sister was right.

From her bedroom window, Grace looked up from the scarlet letters blazing from her 8-Ball and watched the speeding car brake and swerve, mashing Tanner into paste and drifting hard against the fat oak in the neighbour's front yard, a low branch punching through driver's side windshield.

Loud as a Murder

Sarah L. Johnson

A crow glares through the rusted leaves of the birch tree in my front yard. It's Tuesday morning, and I'm looking out the window, waiting for my package. The crow probably isn't glaring at me. It's just a crow. It probably isn't glaring at all. But it sure feels that way, like a message. A scolding.

I like Tuesday mornings, and the reason why is because I'm in love with the UPS guy. Before that, I was infatuated, and I know the difference. I'm smart, but I have difficulty speaking. Strangers usually think I'm deaf. Then they start talking really slow and loud, like that's helpful. Someone famous said it's better to keep your mouth shut and be thought a fool, than to speak and remove all doubt. That guy must have been smart too.

Outside the wind stirs up little cyclones of fallen leaves that whirl out of my yard and into the yard of my next-door neighbors, Mrs. and Mr. Todd. I'll rake them up soon. The leaves, not the Todds.

I get to see Dev, the UPS guy, every Tuesday morning, unless there's a problem. Sometimes there are problems. That's when I call the depot. I have the supervisor's extension number. Buford is his name. Buford understands my difficulty with delays. He thinks I'm crazy, but I'm not crazy, or deaf. I'm autistic. High functioning. Low functioning. Depends on the day.

On good days when I ride the bus to the grocery store or the movies, I can force myself not to flap my hands, or bounce on the balls of my feet, or talk to myself in a Kermit voice. *Sorry Fozzie, they don't serve food in ninth class.* I can pass for neurotypical, but it wears me out and feels like lying, so I don't leave my house or talk to strangers very much ever.

The brown delivery truck pulls up and stops in front of my house with a gasp of the air brakes. I pick up a white manuscript box from the coffee table. The doorbell rings. I stick a shipping label to the top of the box, careful to make sure there are no wrinkles.

My job is to proofread manuals and textbooks. I won't proofread stories and the reason why is because the narrative is distracting and I make mistakes. My boss Shonda tells me mistakes are okay, but I don't like getting copy returned to me because of errors. I insist on printed manuscripts because studies show fewer errors are overlooked on hardcopy.

I'm taking a long time to answer the door, but Dev knows I'm here so he won't ring the bell again. He's patient and doesn't act like he deserves an award for it. That's part of why I love him.

When I open the door, the wind blows it back hard.

"Whoa, happy Tuesday," says Dev, catching the door before it can hit me in the face. "Blustery morning, yeah?"

Over the gale I hear the smile in his voice, but I'm looking at his feet, laced up in sturdy boots. I move my gaze upward over the white socks showing at the tops of his boots, smooth brown calves, and delicate knees that disappear into the darker UPS-brown shorts. I follow the buttons up his shirt, pausing at the hollow of his throat where little strands of chest hair sneak above his white undershirt.

"Go on," he says. "Eat your heart out."

A joke is how he means it. It's also an idiom. It would be impossible for me to eat my own heart. Finally I work my way up to eye contact. Dev's eyes are nice to look at. Dark, almost black, and soft. Like a dog's eyes are soft.

"You good?"

I do my best to smile. "Yes… I am."

I'm not handsome like Dev. I'm not bald with skin problems, and I'm not fat either because I do my exercise on the treadmill every day. I'm also clean, because I take a shower after doing my exercise. But I don't have big soft eyes and beautiful brown skin that shimmers like there's gold underneath. Not like him.

Dev glances at the crow in the tree. "Friend of yours?"

For some reason I say the first dumb thing that comes into my head. "It… doesn't like me."

Dev frowns. "How could anyone not like you? It's probably me she doesn't like."

I want to ask how he knows the crow is a 'she', but I'll never get that many words out.

"Sign here," Dev says, same as every week. It's a script. I like scripts. I say them in my head all the time. *Hi-ho, Kermit the Frog here…* I sign Dev's machine and hand it back to him. He hands me one box. I hand him another. He scans the label with his machine and then tugs at the brim of his UPS cap. "See you next week, buddy."

My name isn't Buddy. He just means it like we're friends. He knows my name is Henry Graham. It's on the shipping label. I don't know Dev's last name. He doesn't wear a label. I do know he has a beautiful body, a sweet smile, and I think about him a lot in the shower. That's the infatuation part.

Dev waves as he heads down the sidewalk. I try to say 'bye' but it jams in my throat and turns into a weird ball of sound that isn't even a word anymore. A gust of wind stings my eyes and rips a shower of orange leaves from the birch. The crow is still there, her clawed feet digging for purchase in the white bark.

I carry my package down the hall into my office. The wind screams around my house like a monster baby so I take the construction earmuffs out of my desk drawer and put them on. Then I split the tape on the white box with my letter opener.

I don't know if Dev is attracted to me. I don't even know if Dev is a faggot. I do know 'faggot' is not a nice word and I don't say it out loud ever, but it's the word my inside voice always uses. The reason why is my dad. He used to drink a lot of alcohol and call me a retard and a faggot. At the time I was too young to understand what those things were. Now I'm almost thirty and I know I'm not retarded, but I am a faggot. Mom says being gay is fine. So does Dad. He doesn't drink alcohol anymore, but the script is set.

The problem is where to go from here. I'm not a virgin, but there's a reason I haven't had a date in five years. Why would someone like Dev be interested in a dweeb with sensory issues whose attempts at speech usually end in a lock-jawed gurgle? I'm a realist. Even I don't want to work that hard for sex.

"It's not easy being green," I mutter in the Kermit voice.

I lift the lid on the box and the stink of scorched paper fires up my nostrils. I recoil so hard I nearly tip my chair over. Covering my nose with my hand I peer into the box. No evidence of fire. Only a pristine title page that says *The 2019 Pocket Guide to Pre-owned Cars*. The smell is gone. My nose feels hot inside. I have one week to complete the proof.

I place the manuscript face down on my desk and flip over the last page. Then I use my window tool, a ruler with a slot cut out in the middle, to isolate the last few lines on the page and work my way to the top. Working backwards is the trick. That way I don't get caught up in the narrative. Even car audio instructions have a narrative, otherwise they don't make sense.

I don't have a car, but I have a stereo in my living room. I listen to different things on it. AC/DC for chores, and Skrillex when I do my exercise on the treadmill beside the couch. I also like Taylor Swift.

I don't listen to music when I work. Proofreading requires concentration. Otherwise you start speaking for the book instead of letting the book speak for itself. Your brain automatically corrects spelling, spacing, punctuation, and inserts the missing words because that's what it expects to see.

Through my window tool I concentrate on the last few lines of the new manuscript.

When tempteD, remember the wOrst mistake you caN make is tO pull ouT your waLlet and purchasE a car on a whim. The informaTion in tHis guIde will give you peace of Mind knowing you've Invested your moNey wisely.

Yeesh. A depreciating asset is hardly a wise investment, but that's narrative and therefore not my department. The scattered caps, however, are. Some style guides allow capitalization for emphasis. I don't care for that. Capitals are loud. I don't like shouting. I use my window as a straight edge to strike out the offending words. I press my blue pencil too hard and the lead breaks, creating a dark blotch in the middle of my perfect line.

"Heya," Dev says, when I open the door. "Happy Tuesday."

I nod, travelling up from his feet to his face. I don't have a box to give him because I finished the car guide early and took it to the UPS store myself. Variation in routine is important if not always pleasant. The people at the UPS store are strangers, but I make sure the box already has a shipping label. Most of their questions can be answered nonverbally.

There's no sign of the crow today, and only a few frost shriveled leaves still cling to the birch tree. Soon Dev will trade in his brown shorts for brown pants. I'll miss his beautiful knees during the snowy months.

Dev gently pushes his machine into my hands. "Gonna sign for me?"

"Oh, right." I take the stylus and scribble something like a signature. "Sorry, I didn't mean to be rude. I was daydreaming."

"Well, how about that?" He hands me a white box. "He speaks."

He's right, my mind wandered and the words slipped out. Of course now I can't make a peep, so I shrug.

Dev's black eyebrow arches. "Are you a writer?"

"Proof… proofreader."

"Bet you read some interesting stuff."

I nod.

"Gotta read carefully, yeah? Catch all the mistakes."

I nod and shift foot to foot. It's all I can do not to bounce up and down. This is way off script. Dev stares at me with those dark eyes. Curious, I think. Or not. Faces are hard for me to read.

He tugs on the brim of his brown cap. "See you next week, buddy."

I step onto the porch as he heads down the sidewalk. "Have… have a good afternoon."

He grins and leaps like an impala into his truck. I give myself a mental high-five.

In my office I don't take out my earmuffs. It's not windy today, so it's a good day to rake leaves. Mine and my neighbor's, Mrs. and Mr. Todd, I also mow their lawn in the summer, and shovel their snow in the winter, and the reason why is because they're old. Mrs. and Mr. Todd have been married a long time, and I suppose that means they're in love, but like a lot of married people they don't act like it. Mrs. Todd sometimes makes a bad face at Mr. Todd, like she's thinking bad things.

I slice through the tape and open the box. No smell this time. Just a title page that reads, *The 2019 Pocket Guide to Pre-owned Cars.*

Shonda always writes a note if there are problems. I pull the stack of paper out of the box and flip through the pages. No note, but even a cursory glance shows multiple errors I've overlooked. Extra spaces, rogue commas – is that an exclamation mark? I always catch exclamation marks. I've made it my mission in life to blue pencil those shouty bastards out of existence.

I drop the brick of paper on my desk. *Whump*, it says, hitting the varnished oak. I've never made this many mistakes in a single manuscript. Is Shonda angry? I'm an adult. I need my job to pay my mortgage. Also, I don't want to lose my regular appointment with UPS, and Dev. Strained clicking noises come from my throat, the ghosts of aborted words rattling their chains. *You know that's the first thing to go on a frog, his tongue...*

I think about emailing Shonda, but she wouldn't have sent it back if she didn't want it done over. I don't like confrontation. I'll redo the proof. This time I'll be extra careful.

My eyes blur and I start to cry a little, which I really hate and only do when extremely frustrated. I'm good at one thing. One. Thing. Of all the tasks I perform on a regular basis, proofreading is the one thing I know I'm not going to fuck up. But this manuscript is a disaster.

I turn the thing face down and flip over the last page.

*When ~~tempteD~~, remember the ~~wOrst~~ mistake you ~~caN~~ make is ~~tO~~ pull ~~ouT~~ your ~~waLlet~~ and ~~purchasE~~ a car on a whim. The ~~informaTion~~ in ~~tHis~~ guide will ~~gIve~~ you peace of **Mind** knowing you've **Invested** your ~~moNey~~ wisely.*

The words weren't bolded. I'm sure they weren't, but they must have been because that's my blue pencil. Only I use a blue pencil. Shonda uses red pen. How I know it's my blue pencil is because I can see the spot where my lead broke and left a blotch.

A shrill caw punctures my concentration. I glance up into the glare of the sun through the blinds. The crow is back, flapping her wings and making a racket. I put on my earmuffs.

I haven't heard from Shonda. I figure everything is okay. But I'm standing in the living room bouncing on my feet and flapping my hands, casting crazy shadows everywhere. It's Tuesday and ten minutes to noon. Dev hasn't rung my doorbell yet.

"Hi-ho, Kermit the Frog here…Hi-ho, and welcome back to the Muppet show… Hi-ho…"

The monotonous recitation does nothing to calm me. Damn, damn, damn. I grab my phone and stare at it. I know I shouldn't call. I know I shouldn't. It's still technically Tuesday morning.

Fuck it, I'm calling.

UPS's electronic voice goes through the options, asking me to state my request, but I can't yet talk so I use the buttons to punch in the extension number. I wait and breathe, trying to relax my throat. I peer out the window. Still no delivery truck, but the crow is there, perched on the bony white branches of the tree.

"Hello, Henry," says Buford in the kind of voice only a man named Buford can have.

"Hi... hello, Buford."

"I've got the manifest right here. Your package went on the truck. It'll be there soon."

"It's... nearly... noon..."

"It's on Elliot's truck. It'll be there."

Elliot? Who the hell is Elliot and why the hell does he have my package? Was Dev fired? Did he quit? Change routes? Take a vacation? Why wouldn't he tell me? I have a terrible feeling about this.

"You all right today, Henry?"

I try to speak, to elucidate, to communicate the seriousness of the situation. I slap the wall and squeeze my eyes shut, but the only sound that makes it out of my mouth is a tight rasp.

"Take your time," Buford says.

This is why I like Buford. He doesn't treat me like a nuisance. He waits. He doesn't try to put his own slow loud words in my mouth either. Like Dev, Buford wants me to speak for myself.

"I'm... worried... very worried..." I trail off as the doorbell rings.

"That what I think it is?"

I didn't hear the air brakes but I glance through the blinds and see the brown truck. "Yes... it is... thank you, Buford... I really app... appreciate..."

"It's no bother, Henry."

I hang up the phone and race for the door.

"Happy Tuesday..." Dev pauses. "You all right, buddy?"

I bypass the boots, the knees, the brown buttons and everything, going straight for his face. "Who... who's E-Elliot?"

Dev smiles, but it's a sad smile. No, not sad. Worried, maybe? Confused? Weirded out... people have too many damn facial expressions. There should be three, or four, no more than four. That would make things easier.

"Buford said... said Elliot..." a low whinny in my chest heralds the death of my words.

"Elliot caught your package by mistake. I nabbed it off his truck. Haven't had time to put it in the system is all." The crow squawks and Dev looks up. "She's watching over you."

"Sh... she's... noisy."

"I bet." He checks his watch. "Hey, sorry I'm late. I know that's rough for you."

"It's okay... I don't mind," I say, a total lie because it clearly isn't and I clearly do. "It's rough... but I don't mind."

Dev winks. "That so?"

I don't always catch on to innuendo – okay, I rarely catch on ever – but I catch this one and my face feels like it's on fire. Maybe it's because I'm so embarrassed I don't care anymore, but the door between my brain and vocal cords swings wide open as I reach for the machine. "I can sign for that if you want."

Our fingers touch. He's wearing gloves but it feels electric. I scribble and he offers me the white box. I hesitate.

"Just paper," Dev says. "It's not going to bite."

Cardboard slides cool and slick into my hands. "You must think I'm the biggest freak."

Dev reaches out, giving me time to step away if I want to. When I don't, he rests his gloved hand on my shoulder and pulls me forward until we're closer than we've ever been before, only a cold white box between us.

"There are worse things," he says. "Don't forget that."

I stand in my open door, watching him leap into his truck. Then I glide down the hall to my office. Something happened. Nothing I can put words to, but something happened, and I'm so happy. I cut the tape on the box, lift the lid and find *The 2019 Pocket Guide to Pre-owned Cars.*

I push away from the desk leaving the manuscript in its box. *No, I don't think so, Miss Piggy.*

I pick up my phone and thumb out an email to Shonda asking what she wants me to do with this fucking manuscript. Except I don't say fuck. It's not a nice word and I usually don't say it out loud ever, or put it in emails to Shonda. I'm respectful. I just find it weird that she hasn't said anything.

After sending the email, I go outside and rake up the leaves on my lawn, and Mrs. and Mr. Todd's, and stuff them into clear plastic bags – the leaves, not the Todds – which takes hours and then I'm too tired to do anything but make a grilled cheese sandwich. My manuscript – and I do think of it as mine – stays on the desk behind the closed office door.

I switch on my stereo and select a Taylor Swift CD. I like her songs about white dresses, kissing in the rain, and all her ex-boyfriends. I've never had a boyfriend. Taylor Swift doesn't speak too highly of the experience. I lie on the couch and doze off to her sweet twangy voice.

In my dream I'm standing in my office at nighttime and it's dark but not really. There's light coming through the window, but not regular light. Red light, like the kind in a photographer's dark room. Dark and red. On my desk there's a pile of ashes. I smell smoke, and I hear myself talking. My voice, but not my voice.

Hi-ho, welcome back to the Muppet Show. And now, as threatened, we proudly present the punishment for everything you did right. The radiant, the all-consuming, LOVE! Take it awaaaaaay!

Instead of applause from a crowd, or jokes from two old men in a balcony, it's a crow in a naked birch tree. A single crow cawing loud as a murder. *Caw, caw caw...*

Thump, thump, thump. I sit up on the couch. Dizzy. Drowsy. Someone knocked on my door. I think. It's dark so I can't see the cars through the living room blinds. I'm not expecting anyone. My parents always call first. Maybe they did call. My phone is locked in the office with that horrible manuscript. I wait for whomever it is to knock again but they don't. Maybe that's why I get up and open the door.

"Hi... Hello."

Dev stands on my front porch, haloed by orange light from the street lamps. This isn't UPS Dev. This is sneakers, jeans, and long black coat Dev. No cap either. His dark hair is neatly combed without looking dorky like mine does when I comb it. His smile is different too. Nervous, maybe.

"I, uh… figured I'd know what to say by the time I got here." Non-regulation Dev shoves his gloveless hands into his coat. "You seem kinda blue lately."

I rub my hands over my face and hold out my arms, examining my skin for a blue tint, which is a sign of hypoxia, or cyanide poisoning, or blood loss. How I know is because I proofed a paramedic training manual one time.

Dev grips my shoulder again. "I meant blue like sad, or depressed."

"Oh." Just when I think I've got a handle on idioms. I feel stupid, but it's mitigated by Dev's bare hand on my shoulder. "D'you want… to want… to…"

He steps back. "It's okay, Henry. Take your time."

I nod and breathe, visualizing unrestricted airflow through my vocal cords. "Would you like to come in?"

We sit across from each other at the kitchen table, not talking and not drinking the tea I made because it's polite to offer guests a hot beverage on a cold day. His skin glows with gold undertones and his obsidian eyes hold mine prisoner. Outside the wind starts to howl.

Dev comes around to my side of the table and pulls me to my feet. I walk my fingertips up the column of his throat to rest against the rough grain of his jaw. We don't say anything. We don't need to.

I kiss him, or he kisses me. What matters is we're kissing. Then we're moving. Down the hall, past the closed office door, into my room. Clothes rustle, tug, and snap, and we're skin-to-skin on my bed. It's so dark I can't see my hand in front of my face, and between the soughing wind, the body heat, and his weight crushing the breath from me, it's like we're twins tangled together in a giant womb, blind and grasping, our shared blood circuit hooked into an enormous heart beating somewhere above us.

Dev utters an incoherent stream of words I don't recognize in a looping lulling rhythm. It's a script. I like scripts. And I love the sound of his voice chanting endlessly in the black.

"Stay," he whispers into my neck. "Stay with me. Stay…"

"It's my house. Where would I go?" I find the words so easily I feel as though I could talk the ears off a herd of African elephants. How's that for an idiom? But I don't talk, and the reason why is that my mouth is busy doing other things.

"You're too good, Henry. Too good. I had to come."

And he does. We both do. Then we sleep.

It's still dark when I wake up, and I don't know what time it is because I left my phone across the hall in my office and I can't have a regular alarm clock otherwise I stay up all night watching the numbers change. I'm weird that way.

Dev sleeps beside me, his arm heavy on my chest. I carefully slide out of bed and go to the kitchen for a glass of water. I drink my water, leave the glass in the sink and head back down the hall. I pause outside my bedroom door. Part of me thinks I dreamed it all. When I go back in my room, my bed will be empty. I hear a muffled ding. Instead of going back to bed I go into my office and pick up my phone. I have one email.

Hi Henry,

I was surprised to hear from you so soon after getting your note about taking a long vacation. Regardless, I'm not sure which manuscript you're talking about. I don't think we've ever bought a used car guide.

If you're ready for more work, I've got several projects I could use you on. Maybe send that manuscript back and I'll see if I can sort it out.

-Shonda

I put the phone down on the desk. Red light bleeds through the blinds onto my manuscript. And it is mine. I know that now.

"Hey, sleepwalker."

I turn around to find Dev standing in the doorway, robed in red-black shadows.

"There is no... muh... manuscript."

He points to the window where the outline of a black bird sits on a skeletal tree branch. "She can't stop me, but she does require that I warn you."

"Warn?"

"There are rules governing my nature as there are rules governing yours. See for yourself."

He points to the desk. I turn around and the manuscript I left in the box because I was too 'blue' to face more errors, is now out of the box, facedown on my desk, with the last page flipped over, bathed in bloody light.

When ~~tempteD~~*, remember the* ~~wOrst~~ *mistake you* ~~caN~~ *make is* ~~tO~~ *pull* ~~ouT~~ *your* ~~waLlet~~ *and* ~~purchasE~~ *a car on a* *whim. The ~~informaTion~~ in ~~tHis~~ guide will ~~gIve~~ you peace of ~~Mind~~ knowing you've ~~Invested~~ your ~~moNey~~ wisely.*

It's obvious now. I talked when I should have listened. I wrote when I should have read. So caught up in what I thought was correct that I made a mistake, and this time it's not okay.

"Underhanded, I admit," he says. "The warning has to speak for itself, but people see what they want, and there's no rule against using that to my advantage."

"Narrative… not my department."

Dev shrugs. "I gave you three chances. In writing."

"What are you?"

"Love," he said. "Concentrated, personified, manifested. I'm what people search for their whole lives. Most are lucky enough not to find it."

I pull my arms into my chest and rock back and forth the way I haven't done since I was little. On the desk my manuscript blackens and curls into a pile of ashes, filling my office with the smell of burnt paper. Dev's smile gleams like a blade.

"I meant what I said, Henry. You're too good, and I wish you weren't. The truth is no one deserves me more than you do, and no one deserves me less. What's the word for that?"

"Paradox," I say in Kermit's voice.

He reaches for me with a crimson hand, radiant and all consuming, the punishment for everything I did right. There are worse things than being a lonely freak. But I can't complain. I let him in.

Skin Deep

Robert Bose

Thank you, Jordan, for your interest in Skin Deep[1]! If you are having second, sober thoughts, or were signed up against your will, we would direct your attention to Article 1, Clause 1[2] below. Please take your time; Skin Deep prides itself on transparency and does not condone keeping our beloved clients in the dark and feeding them shit[3] like our less reputable competitors[4].

No complaints? Excellent. Welcome aboard.

As you are no doubt aware, Jordan, Skin Deep is a premium service, providing personalized matchmaking between your inner monster and our

---

[1] Skin Deep is a wholly owned subsidiary of Monster Match, a Factory owned and operated personal services corporation.
[2] Upon perusal of this legally binding document, Skin Deep places an irrevocable lien on the applicant's soul, with discharge conditions set on whimsy and forfeiture upon complaint.
[3] Unless requested.
[4] Meatups, Fleshmates, and Growlr.

stable[5] of exceptional young[6] ladies[7]. We are here for you, to serve your needs. By monsters, for monsters, a philosophy reflected in our new[8] motto[9], Conplectere Monstrum Interiorem.

Do you embrace your inner monster, Jordan?[10] Of course you do, you're here aren't you? Pulled your oozing ego up to the incel's all you can eat buffet, unloved[11] and rage filled, flailing your metaphysical tentacles in the wind, thrusting your less than average sized penis into your covertly purchased M69 sex doll, ironically named Charity.

Relax, Jordan. We understand. You're a nice guy. And we are here to help.

You are undoubtedly asking yourself, as you find your bedroom door sealed shut and phone non-functional, about the price, and more importantly, the process. Our fee, we are pleased to announce, has

---

[5] Not a traditional barn.

[6] At heart.

[7] Self identified. Skin Deep is an equal opportunity employer, priding itself on diversity, and as such, each lady, while definitely a monster, may, or may not exhibit traditional female attributes.

[8] Feedback revealed the old motto, Caveat Emptor, sent the wrong message.

[9] Motto required as per the Purgatory-Vatican cooperation treaty of 1627.

[10] A rhetorical question, no actual answer required.

[11] Except by your mother. And Troy.

been paid[12], so release that concern unless you desire one or more items from our secret menu[13].

The monster within you requires coaxing to materialize. The process is simple. Your skin is peeled, from head to toe, inch by inch, to reveal your true, monstrous self. It sounds painful, and it is, but tell us Jordan, what is pain, except unreleased pleasure? Most, if not all, of our previous customers[14] have expressed some small concern during the process, but rest assured, all received the ultimate happy ending.

By now you probably hear chittering and/or slithering in your hallway, and are catching a hint of old tomb in the air. Don't get up, Jordan. She'll let herself in.

---

[12] By a well funded Kickstarter. You remember Lisa don't you? She remembers you.

[13] Menu available upon request.

[14] Between 75-80%, with some small standard deviation.

Red Door

Sarah L. Johnson

I backed out of the pristine hell of Starbucks into an earthy breeze circulating through the mall. KJ stood, furiously texting, by a trashcan littered with cottonwood fluff. I handed her a cup. "Night Blooming Tulip iced tea."

"Of course." She tucked her phone into her shirt and examined the beverage. Sunlight burned through the exposed breasts of the mermaid logo, turning the black tea a bloody red. "You always go for the weirdest thing."

"My zest for life."

"Hot barista recommended it?"

"Pink hair and the voice of an angel." I eyed the outline of her phone through her nursing bra. "This was supposed to be a Girl's Day."

"Here we go."

"No husbands, no babies."

"She's teething, Soph. It's been rough."

"I'm sure daddy'll survive an afternoon of single parenthood."

"Don't be a bitch, okay?"

"You promised." The words curled off my tongue like bitter orange peels.

"I was just checking in," she huffed. "That's what you do when you're a partner... and a mother."

"Fine." I stepped back. Weeks it took to get KJ out of the house sans kidloaf. I didn't want to fuck it up with our usual circular argument. Judging by the way she fired a straw into her cup, smashing through bergs of crushed ice, it wasn't over yet. She held a sip in her mouth before swallowing with a slight wince.

"Christ," I said. "Spit it out."

Her eyes nailed into mine. "You're not getting any younger."

"Rude." I gulped from my own cup and nearly gagged. What the hell Starbucks? Another thing that should have been sweet and fun. Somehow spoiled. "You told me I look like a twenty-year-old stripper in those fish leather pants."

"You should have bought those." KJ dutifully sipped her foul weed drippings. "But we're forty, not twenty. Why are you wasting time with a married guy?"

"Tom wants to be married and I don't want to be. I call that perfect."

"I call it adultery."

"And I'm forty. You're forty-three."

Her forehead knotted. "You don't care that it's not going anywhere?"

"Where does it have to go?"

She glanced at her watch. "You'll see it differently when you get swept off your feet by prince charming."

"Or the big bad wolf," I said with a wink. "Not everyone wants the nuclear fantasy."

My words blighted her smile and her body shrunk in on itself, sharp corners rounded off by the sanding belt of domesticity. Changed, but so much the same. Katherine Jane and Sophie. Best friends. Her five-year gay summer and the love of my life – until she left me for some business bland in a Toyota.

"Don't look at me that way," I protested.

"How's it gonna work with Tom? Y'know, long term?"

"How does anything work long term?"

"You always answer a question with a question. You're so secretive."

"I'm evasive, there's a difference. And why are your questions more valid than mine?"

"I asked first."

KJ only asked when she already knew my answers. Or thought she did.

We wandered through the outdoor shopping plaza, down an arcade lined with trees, and steel and glass art installations, lightly spotted from spring rain. The air licked over us, wet with bruised leaves and low clouds. My mind strayed to Tom. Maybe I chose him because it couldn't go anywhere. Because he couldn't go anywhere. He was an anchor, holding me in place for as long as I cared to be held. Until something called me away.

I looked around for another trash can, my unsettled stomach refusing to accept another swallow of dank ditch water.

"Food hall?" KJ asked with a hopeful nudge. I'd promised her poutine before day's end. She'd get the traditional and pull faces at my cheesy chicken hearts or whatever strange offering caught my eye. And then, finally, I could tell her. Until then, I refused to think about it.

"There's a place I want to check out first," I said, scanning the store fronts. "A lingerie shop."

"Since when are you the type?"

"Since I wear panties on occasion. And you need a real bra."

She pulled her cardigan closed. "I'm nursing."

"Kid's almost a year old and has teeth. You don't need to wear the milking harness twenty-four seven."

Instead of lacing into me, she laughed. "Assuming they have anything big enough to contain these weather balloons. Where is it?"

"The barista gave me directions. Said it's kind of hidden, not even in the mall directory."

"Another secret for your collection." KJ shook the ice in her cup. "Though if this tea is any indication of her taste…"

We found it at the far end of the mall, sandwiched between a frozen yogurt shop and a butcher's. An alley, too narrow for deliveries. High on the stucco wall was an odd symbol enclosed in a circle, and a diagonal arrow, pointing into the alley. In and down. The alley itself dead ended with a plain red door.

"There's no sign," KJ said.

"Hmm."

"There's no handle."

I pushed. The warm wood under my palms didn't give.

"Sophie, wait—" she said as I knocked.

Paint freckled my knuckles. Red. Like poppies. But liquid. Melted. Sunset on a flat lake. Red you could drown in.

KJ grabbed my hand. "Let's go."

"Wait a sec. Let's see if someone answers."

"I don't want to, Soph."

I couldn't look away. From the door. From that red.

KJ tugged. "How about fro-yo? Bet they've got a weird flavour... like Cuban Cigar or Hot Dog Water—"

The door swung inward with a sound like a woman's soft cry, enough light falling through the aperture to reveal a small patch of red and purple tile.

"Nuh uh," KJ said.

"Oh yes." I pulled her after me and we nearly fell into the darkness, my arms flying out, instinctively searching for solid walls, anything steady. The door shut behind us. KJ pressed up behind me, thumbs sliding into the groove between my lower ribs. She knew my body that well. Still.

A light flicked on above us, illuminating the small vestibule enclosed by red velvet drapes. One of the curtains swished and a woman swanned out.

"Ladies." She spoke in a voice as sumptuous as the velvet, her dark skin glowing under the dim light. "Welcome to Red Door."

My stomach wobbled and my toes tried to splay in my ballet flats as my brain and body struggled against contradicting sensory input. The floor wasn't just uneven, it was sloped. KJ slid up beside me in the strange half-dark, her form partially swallowed by the crowding shadows. She swayed, disoriented as I was by how the curtains killed the overhead glow on contact and I wondered... How much of what we are is light? And when it's gone, where do we go?

"Crazy place you got," KJ mumbled, presumably to the woman, but looking at me with eyes blasted open to nothing but black pupil.

Laughter rippled through the silence, like a thick waterfall. "I'm Brinn, and I'll look after you today. Follow me."

We followed Brinn through a gap in the curtains I didn't see, even as we passed through it.

"What's with the fun house effects?" I asked, ignoring KJ's raptor clutch on my arm.

"Red Door is special," Brinn replied, leading us down a short corridor, reasonably lit, but nowhere near retail strength. "Passing through means leaving the world behind."

"Kinda heavy, for a lingerie boutique?"

Brinn abruptly pivoted on one exquisitely booted toe. "*You* found the door, Sophie. Don't tell me *you* expected something conventional behind it."

My spinal cord quivered. "How do you know my name?"

Brinn smiled, teeth like pearls against the pink oyster flesh of her lips. "Your cup."

I glanced down at the sloshing iced tea in my hand, my name typed on the label. KJ's cup was empty. Typical. She consumed her Starbucks down to the last ice cube, chewing them. I hated the sound. And I hated the way Brinn said *you*. Like she knew things about me. Like she'd been waiting. KJ wanted to leave – that KJ's instincts were almost always right followed as an afterthought.

"If you're looking for something more… familiar," Brinn said, "there's a Victoria's Secret, right by Crate & Barrel."

Goddamn fighting words. I stiffened my shoulders. "Didn't expect a tilted stage, that's all."

TERRACE VII: WALL OF FIRE

Brinn led us through a second curtained doorway into a cozy room smelling faintly of roses, dominated by a fireplace big enough to stand in, piled with glowing embers and low flames behind an iron grate. I scanned the walls, covered in paintings, and mirrored alcoves featuring curious sculptures, realist and abstract, all depicting the feminine form. Curved hips, cradled waists, pebble-tipped sweep of breasts, spine arching into the distinctive female slope of neck and jaw. Acrylic paint vulvas so built up as to be three dimensional. Genitally suggestive inkblots intermingled with an assortment of womb-like chalices. All of it red, with not a single pair of undies in sight.

"Nice gallery," I said, without a shred of sarcasm.

"Have a seat," Brinn said. "Get comfortable. I'll be right back."

I settled on the overstuffed leather sofa, implanting like a fertilized egg. KJ snuggled in next to me. "This place is a trip."

"Right?" I said. "That entryway, the hall."

"Felt like being born."

"Only thing I feel is vertigo."

"That weird tea." She rubbed her belly. "Can't believe you didn't drink it. You're the adventurous one."

I swished my full cup. "Some adventures taste like ass."

"She's been gone a while."

Silence settled over us like a weighted blanket. In the fireplace an ember popped and pinged off the grate. The flames dipped lower. Still no Brinn. How long had she been gone? No windows, no clocks, and neither KJ nor I reached for our phones. I did feel removed, isolated, enveloped. Even the thought of my phone's existence was only the briefest speck of dust moting across my mental landscape. I zoned out in the fading firelight. KJ's weight molded against me, heavy and radiating heat. She'd passed out. The sleepy scent of her diffused around us. Salty skin, recent shampoo, and a faint trace of the cigarettes I knew she'd started sneaking again but her husband didn't. She smelled like a nice girl in a dive bar at a bad hour. I breathed her in, all of her, until she was part of me.

My eyelids slid lower and I realized I was about to drop my cup. The nearest trash bin was across the room, crowded to the brim with empty Starbucks cups. Since when did the mermaid have tits? Or did she always, and I just never noticed?

Brinn returned, pulling a rack with a single garment bag hanging from it. "Took me a few minutes to find what I was looking for."

I glanced down at the top of KJ's head and the tip of her nose. "Felt longer."

"Gestational isolation." Brinn squeezed my shoulder. "Peaceful, isn't it?"

"Starting to think we'd been abandoned."

"Are you often left behind, Sophie?"

What the hell was that supposed to mean? When I didn't answer, Brinn reached down, tickling KJ under her chin. "Wake up, beautiful."

KJ wriggled and I shivered as the comparative chill slipped into the pockets of space between our bodies.

"Soph?" she mumbled.

I lassoed an arm around her shoulders. "I'm here."

"Sorry... baby's keeping me up at night," she said, rubbing her eyes.

Brinn took a seat on the chair across from us. "Sleep is trust. Rare and primal. Honour that."

As if she'd sung an incantation, a terrible thirst came over me. I lifted my straw to my lips, dipped my tongue down to the floor of my mouth creating a depression for something bitter and vegetative. What I got was more like metal, sour and corroded. Brinn's smile hardened, eyes like ink in the warm light. I smiled back, brought the straw to my lips again, and subtly as I could, spit the tea back.

"Night Blooming Tulip isn't for everyone." Brinn plucked the cup from my hand and dropped it in the trash with the others.

"Interesting art," KJ said, gaze roving over the frameless canvases. Swirls of visceral pink and red, darkening into a wet organ-hot black.

Brinn rose from her seat. "Red Door is a patron."

"They look like innards," I said.

"Self-reflection is vital." Brinn traced one finger along a scarlet uterine bulb sculpture beside the fireplace. "To examine with our senses, and our reason, what we nurture within. You like this one, don't you Sophie?"

In fact, I did. The shape, the meaty pigment.

"Tell me," Brinn asked, like a yawn compelling an echo.

"It's calm, like a place... a place I can't stay." The words tumbled out, the way truth does, when you open its cage.

"What?" KJ accused, eyes lagging behind the swivel of her head.

"No, this is good," Brinn said. "We're getting somewhere."

"Thought this was a lingerie store," KJ slurred. "Fancy panties an' intimate... apparel."

Brinn trained her dark gaze on me. "What's more intimate than a secret? We wear them next to our skin, they carry our heat, and our scent. They want to be known. And keeping them gives us power."

"Sophie's sleepin' with a married guy," KJ blurted in a muddled slop of sound.

"Hey!" I snapped.

"Is that your secret, Sophie? That you're ashamed, or thrilled?"

I shook my head. "Neither, I don't even... he's no one."

KJ snorted. How dare she judge? She left me. To get married and have a baby, relegating me to an inert pocket of her life. Where I couldn't hurt her anymore.

"I wanna see..." KJ's voice didn't fade so much as it dissolved.

"KJ?" I jostled her shoulder, and when she didn't respond I snapped my fingers in front of her face.

"Hey, you with me?" I pressed my hand to her forehead. "You're really warm."

Her head dropped against my chest, scalding me as she slid her arms around my waist hugging me hard. A soft milky scent drifted up from her. Then wet.

"Fuck." KJ plucked her blouse. "Oh my god…"

"No need to be self-conscious," Brinn said. "Our bodies respond to nourishing environments."

My mind drifted to the tea, and on some level it made sense that the love hormone would land on the bitter region of my tongue. "Sorry Brinn, but I think we need to go."

"No," KJ said. "Let's see what she brought."

She pointed to the hanging garment bag and curiosity snatched me in its grip before I could decline. With a flourish Brinn unzipped the bag. Instead of lace trim, slippery ribbon, and sheer nylon, it was a white, cap-sleeved, collared blouse, black neck tie, and pleated plaid skirt.

My heart banged in my ears.

"School girl?" I asked, vocal cords quaking. "More of a costume than lingerie."

"Call it what you want," Brinn said. "But tell me how it feels."

"Nothing, I—"

"Cute," KJ said. "Tom'll love it."

"This piece," Brinn said tightly, "and this place, are not for men."

I had to agree. Inside these walls, Tom wasn't a person. He was barely an idea. Inside. He was no longer unnecessary. KJ nodded as though she understood, and maybe she actually did. For once we might be on the same wavelength. A frequency that itched under my skin and made my teeth tingle.

Brinn's smile, hard as tempered glass, reformed as she pulled the hanger off the rack. "Would you like to try it on?"

I shook my head. "We need to go."

I tugged KJ's hand but she didn't move. I turned and tracked her gaze to the enormous fireplace, now vacant of flames. The bricks in the back were gone, replaced by elaborate draping satin, and velvet panels, overlapping and pooling on the floor, and in the middle a dark black slit.

"Fitting room is through there," Brinn said.

"What kind of freak show is this?" I asked, as KJ got halfway across the room before I could catch her arm. "What are you doing?"

She turned to me, glass-eyed. "Grab that get up and come with me."

The fabric panels pulsed, and the slit grew slightly wider, the blackness within not as dark as I'd thought. We approached the fireplace, finding a narrow path cleared through the hearth. Nowhere near as baking hot as it ought to have been. Instead, a humid warmth engulfed us, like steam, like breath. But it still smelled like flames.

KJ towed me along, stepping between velvet panels. "Come on, Soph. This place is a trip, let's find out where."

I was always the one dragging her under bridges, over thinly frozen ponds, and into creepy urban haunts. Safety as an afterthought. Not today.

"Sophie," Brinn said, her voice close as though murmuring in my ear. "What you leave behind is your choice. Dreams or reality. The anchor or the current. Just know that once the Red Door closes, it never opens again."

The bitter metal taste flooded my mouth as KJ's feverish grip on my hand pulled me through the red and into the black. My eyes adjusted. A number of curtained alcoves surrounded a raised platform in the middle of a room even larger than the parlour.

"This is weird," I said.

KJ elbowed my ribs. "Shh."

With a swish, a slender bronze blade of a woman cut through one of the curtains into the low light. She seemed not to notice us as she boosted her naked body onto the platform, scooting back and arching her spine – her shoulders, breasts, and bald head shimmering gold. Another woman stepped from another alcove and joined the first. Then another and another, until I counted half a dozen, ten, twenty. Until I couldn't tell how many separate bodies twined together on the platform.

Tattooed hides or blank canvases, freckles, mahogany, ivory, cellulite, ladder ribs, rounded bellies, flat chests, thick asses, knuckle spines, heavy thighs, gleaming scalp, tumbling curls, flexing muscle with smooth bare cunts, plump tits and hair shadowed cocks. Women of every permutation and combination, weaving together in a moaning tapestry of limbs, skins, and open wet mouths.

I dug my heels in. "I'm getting out of here."

KJ whirled on me. "No."

"Pardon?"

"How many times have I followed you, wherever you wanted to go? How many times have I held you when you were sure you'd fly apart, or fade away?"

"KJ, there is something seriously wrong with this place."

"Does Tom know you're going to rip his heart out and eat it? Because I swear that's all that keeps you alive. Devouring people."

"Jesus, what are you talking about?"

"I'm talking about Sophie, the Great and Terrible." KJ gripped my face in her hands, fingertips like claws.

"I… I'm not…"

"The perfect predator?"

"Nice to know you think so poorly of me."

"Why would I think poorly of a wolf for eating a sheep?" Her thumbs stroked my cheeks, smudging away tears I hadn't felt fall. "I'm not asking you to change, only to stay."

She'd never spoken so frankly. Never called me out this brutally.

"You don't look well," I said.

"Caught yourself in a mirror lately?"

Did I look different? Could she know?

"Just try it on," she said.

TERRACE VII: WALL OF FIRE

My head pounded and I pressed the flocked hanger against my temple. The crisp blouse brushed my cheek. A shimmer of fatigue jellied my knees. An orgy was taking place less than ten feet from us, and all KJ wanted was for me to try on this costume.

"You'll wait for me?"

She popped up on her toes and kissed me. "I'm not the one who leaves."

That's not true at all... An argument could wait. I skirted the passion play on the platform, passing through a cloud of salty sweat, past the soft breath and pale sighs. A tiny foot extended from the edge, hot toes grazing my arm, sending a bolt of lightning through my bones, into my blood, and spidering through my belly like an electrified cage. Strong enough to keep anything that lived inside me from getting out.

Pulling aside the curtain to a changing alcove, I found the elusive mirror absent in any other part of this place. Jeans, t-shirt, and socks hit the floor. I avoided my reflection, not wanting to see myself naked. Exposed and altered. But clothes still looked good on me. The blouse hugged my torso like it was grown for me and the skirt skimmed my hips and thighs before dropping to my knees.

The mirror said it all.

KJ was right, I looked haunted, hunted. And the costume itself... well, it wasn't that sexy. It was a uniform.

And it took me back. To myself.

A budding baby dyke in the tenth grade. June afternoon and a beautiful girl a year ahead kissed me in the magic stairwell. Later I saw her in the hallway, boyfriend's arm looped around her shoulders like a water-swollen rope. She didn't see me, or chose not to. Disastrously tender and hormone saturated, I swallowed five of my mom's valiums with a few slugs of vodka and died.

For a while.

Floating in a void, a place where light – as a concept, wave, or particle – did not exist. Floating in nothing. Not even a body. The flying man thought experiment. Except I could hear and feel the pulse all around me. Steady. Percussive. The heartbeat of the universe.

A hypnotic metronome. A call seeking an answer.

Except I didn't belong. I couldn't stay. Some part of me knew I'd gone too far.

Call it a near death experience. A misfiring nervous system. But I woke up with that drum beat in my head. And it rewired me.

How could Brinn know?

I slung the curtain aside and stepped out as my adolescent self. "Hey, there's something I need to tell you..."

A groan drew my gaze back to the undulating fucktangle on the platform where fingers grew claws, mouths flashed with steely fangs, shoulder blades sprouted leathery wings, spines elongated into tails, and silvery fur spun out of smooth skin.

"KJ?" I called.

A few woman-creatures looked up, pupils glinting like knife points. Like wolves. I slammed back against the brick wall. No sign of KJ. My heart fired like a cannon and my adrenal glands gushed. The tea. I drank some, but KJ drank more. Enough to give her a fever. So why was I hallucinating? I had to be. This wasn't real. Not the soft white blouse, not the women, not the monsters.

"KJ, where the hell are you?"

I frantically scanned between the prowling pile of talons, scales, and wings, finally finding her, crouched by the platform, eyes round and haloed white like occluded moons.

Brinn said I could choose, but I had nothing to leave. Nothing left. Except now, for the first time, I saw in KJ's lunar eyes what she'd always seen in mine. A call to the unknown. To the unknowable.

It was why she left me. My incessant seeking. A need to go somewhere there was no coming back from. And she couldn't follow. She had too much to lose then. And now I did too.

"KJ, please..." I reached out, fingers splayed, hyperextended as though her mind hinged on that extra millimetre. "KJ."

Her gaze slid over me, a twin lunar eclipse.

"Come with me," I pleaded.

A reptilian beauty on the platform unfurled her wings and her tail snaked out. A clawed finger beckoned to KJ.

"No!"

The creature's mane of blue fire swept around in a wave as she turned to me, eyes iridescent with warning and hunger, but strangely lacking in malevolence. I heard her speak, though her mouth did not move.

This is your choice

"Please don't take her."

Choose what you leave behind.

My secret. That dying once left me craving a return, to the heartbeat of the universe. But now there was another heartbeat, and how was I supposed to do this without her? How do you step out of the light that defines you? And when you do, where do you go?

"I can't..."

The creature dropped to her knees, hands resting on her broad thighs, and cocked her head. *You have.*

"KJ..."

She was already climbing onto the platform. Devoured in a living avalanche of flesh. I slapped my way through the heavy fabric panels, surging forward. Until the darkness lifted enough for my vision to swim. Black waving walls. A sloped floor. The vestibule.

I pushed through until my palms struck something that did not give way. A cool hard handle. A twist. A flash of inverted x-ray color. And a light so bright.

A few blinks and my brain caught up to my eyes. Sidewalk, torn awnings, withered trees, red-orange sky, and twisted steel sculptures. Outside.

Whirling around, my hands slapped crumbling beige stucco, where moments ago there'd been an alley, a dead end. A red door. My breath came in harsh animal gasps. I examined my stinging palms and wiped the flecks of crimson paint on my white uniform blouse.

"Fancy seeing you here."

The voice of an angel.

Wobbling, I found myself nose to nose with a girl. Satchel slung over her shoulder, pink hair let down from her messy bun. The barista.

"Y'okay, hon?"

"I got out?" I said, still uncertain.

"Well yeah, you can't stay there," she said, then cocked her head. "Eventually it pushes you out, one side or the other. But you... this is unusual."

Scrubbing my hands over my face, I tried to slide my diverging realities back together. "There was a Red Door. Here. Just like you said."

The girl's eyes narrowed like she was trying to pocket dial 911. Instead she gently gripped my shoulders, inside her wrist I saw a strange symbol enclosed in a circle, like the one at the entrance to the alley that no longer existed.

"Think of it as being born," she said. "Love the birthday suit, by the way."

"My friend."

She shrugged, batting extended eyelashes she didn't need to be beautiful. "Everyone chooses what they leave behind. But I didn't think she'd choose you."

"KJ?"

"Look, I gotta split." She leaned in, whispering. "I'm not supposed to be out and about on this side. But you're a hard soul. You might do okay." She reached out, gently palming my stomach. "Both of you."

The angel's voice faded like a bell as she strolled away, pink hair bouncing. Without choosing a direction, I plodded barefoot along the boulevard where fiery light rained through tattered awnings, and broken storefront windows gaped like mouths full of shattered teeth. A red ribbon blew across the pitted sidewalk, coiling around my ankle before fluttering away on a wind smelling of burnt earth. Beyond the emerald mermaid of Starbucks, massive black gates rose into the sky.

Such Stains

Sarah L. Johnson & Robert Bose

"That god damn dog is shitting on our lawn again,"
said Stacy, glaring through the kitchen window as she
filled the kettle under the faucet. "And she just lets
him."

"There are no bad dogs," Dale replied, sprawled
in his foul cycling gear on their new leather sofa.
"Only bad owners."

"You're half right." She set the kettle to boil and
dumped loose tea into her thermos. Some blend Dale
said promised tranquility and balanced hormones.
"Mrs. Todd is as much of an asshole as her dumb...
whatever kind of mutt that is currently defecating in
my tulips."

"Bichon," Dale yawned. "And Mrs. Todd is a
widow, be nice."

"Her husband went nuts and got run over by a
Winnebago. Doesn't make her a saint."

"He ran into a Winnebago. Big difference."

"She does naked yoga in her bathroom."

"Which looks right into our bathroom."

"She's like a sex doll left out in the sun," said Stacy with a barb of envy. She'd kill to look that good at sixty. She'd kill to look that good now. But covetous thoughts of the neighbor's well-maintained tush were interrupted by the sight of her dog digging up a marigold. "I'm going to slaughter that thing."

"We're doing this again are we?"

"I mean it this time. I'm gonna drown it in a bucket of bleach."

"Well I'm going to feed it to a bear."

"Drop it down a manhole."

"Stuff it in a wasp's nest."

"Put my foot so far up its ass it'll bark out a Nine West kitten heel."

"Smoosh it with a shovel."

Stacy sighed. "Weak."

"Long ride. Tired. Aren't you working tonight?"

Stacy watched Mrs. Todd's cosmetically plumped lips purse. Listened as the faint cooing to her revolting canine travelled across the yard and through the window. Like a wind chime. A horribly sweet earworm that made her teeth ache.

The kettle whistled. Stacy sucked in a breath, realizing she'd gripped the handle of the largest knife in the wooden block next to the sink.

"Babe?"

She jumped, yanking the knife from the block. "Jesus, Dale."

"Whoa!" He backed up, clutching a pint of vegan ice cream.

"You startled me!"

"And that's a stabbing offense?"

She let the knife clatter into the sink. "Fuck, sorry." She wouldn't hurt the dog. It was just an animal, doing what animals do. The killing thing... that was just a game they played. A joke.

Dale's eyebrows cinched together. "You okay, Stace?"

"Actually, no." She swiped one hand under her runny nose and pressed the other to her lower spine. "Heachachey, and my back."

Dale slipped his arm around her waist, kissed her sweaty forehead, and murmured against her temple. "You always get a little nuts this time of the month."

She frowned and wriggled away.

"Aw don't, I didn't mean it like that," he said pulling her back. "Have you been drinking the tea? The barista told me it's great for... female stuff."

She nodded. "Don't feel any more tranquil though."

"Call in sick tonight."

"Can't. Big multi-author event."

"The cozy bookstore isn't going to turn itself into a circus."

"Call me the ringmaster." She cackled like a vaudeville villain, leaning into his solid body. "One of these days I'll come home in a tailcoat and top hat."

"With a riding crop?"

"So demanding."

"Goes with the earrings." He touched a finger to the jeweled stud in her earlobe. A tenth anniversary present. Some kind of clear stone that gradually took on color from your unique body chemistry the longer you wore them. Dale made her promise never to take them out. She hadn't and after a few weeks of wear they were a pale violet.

"Still can't believe *you* came up with such a thoughtful gift," Stacy said.

Dale looked sheepish. "Well actually, they were Mrs. Todd's idea."

"Serious?"

"I wanted something that'd blow your mind. I needed a woman's opinion, and she's got a Factory catalogue subscription."

"Didn't realize you two were that close."

"She's our neighbor, Stace. Our grieving neighbor. Don't tell me you're jealous."

Was she jealous? Of a sixty-year-old widow?

"Hey, could you grab some Nicorette on the way home?" Dale asked, interrupting her stream of doubt. "That, or a pack of Camels."

"So that's why you're hitting the fake ice cream." She ran her fingers through his sweaty hair. "You know I'm proud of you."

He patted his belly, encased in a spandex cycling onesie. "Just gotta burn off the quitter paunch."

"Who says there aren't any fat vegans?" she said, turning to go get dressed, squealing when he yanked her back into his arms.

"You're a crazy bitch, and I love you."

"I'm not crazy," she growled, feeling him smile into her hair as she kissed his neck. "Wait up for me."

Stacy stacked the last folding chair, brushed the people crumbs from her hands, and gathered wine glasses discarded on the book shelves, a crime that made her shudder. Her heel caught on a cracked tile in the kitchen and dregs of red wine pitched out of the glasses, splattering the front of her white dress.

"God damn it." Yet another trip to the dry cleaners. She hated them, giving her that wide-eyed look every month like they'd never seen such stains. But, the clothes always came back spotless.

She fondled an open bottle of the second cheapest plonk. The kind poets drank by the gallon while snapping their fingers between stanzas. The kind that gave her heartburn and nightmares. She ought to have filled her tea thermos with the Red Door gin that Dale got her from some fancy shop in the mall where they would faint at the merest whiff of screw top merlot. Although everything seemed to taste bitter lately. Dale said it was her imagination. That hag Mrs. Todd mentioned peri-menopause. Maybe she was getting sick. With shaking hands she drank from the bottle as her boss emerged from the back room. He patted her arm and started cashing out. He didn't say anything. He didn't have to.

What a night. Dreadful readings interspersed with a band so generic she couldn't remember its name. People buying books they'd never read, determined to support lost causes. The evening stretched and stretched, breaking when a middle-aged woman with a nervous laugh read a terrible children's story. About fairies. At some point Stacy heard music. Faint, but definitely music. A dissonant chime scratching her ear drum, wriggling its way into her brain and boring a maze through her thoughts.

One thought was clear, however. The music. No one else heard it.

"Oh for..." Stacy tripped through the front door, first over the cycling shoes and then the actual damn bicycle. "Ow, fuck sakes, Dale?"

"Didn't want to leave it outside," Dale said rounding the corner. "Never know who's wandering the streets at night." He helped her out of the thicket of his cycling accoutrements. "Have you been drinking? You smell like a Real Housewife."

"Don't bust my balls, okay?" She kicked off her shoes, rolled down her thigh highs and tossed them over Dale's bike. "I took an Uber home."

"No gum?"

"You were less needy when you smoked."

Dale flinched like a wounded lamb in his micro fleece jammies. "I'm going to make you a cup of tea."

Stacy was about to take a hard pass on that godawful tea when the faintest strains of chimes rang out. She rushed past Dale into the living room, the sound growing louder. A song. That same song. She scanned the room from the sofa to the coffee table, to the dark television and back again. "Where's that music coming from?"

"What?" Dale said behind her.

She whirled on him. "Don't you hear it?" She swiped his phone off the sofa, trying not to squint at what was most certainly a stain from that garbage vegan ice cream. "Were you watching or listening to something?"

"Nosy much?" He plucked the phone from her hand as she caught a blur of text followed by wolf and heart emojis. "I was reading lube reviews if you wanna know, and they don't exactly have a soundtrack. But check out this video of epic chafing pics."

He came up behind her, sliding his arms over her shoulders and holding the phone out so they could both see. Images of raw abraded flesh assaulted Stacy's eyes as the song's swaying cadence filled her head, shivering like a snare drum. Shredded skin. Clotting beads of blood. The song kicked down her spine, pounding in her lower back and belly. Like a mallet. Hard, hot, and angry. A weapon built to smash. And it made her feel... powerful.

She spun around. "I'm sorry."

"Hey," he cried when she knocked the phone out of his hand and it landed on the hardwood with an ominous thwack.

"Let's not fight." She coiled her arms around his neck, kissing him.

"I wasn't fighting. You came home, forgot my gum, and shit all over me."

"I said I'm sorry."

He sighed and kissed her back. "Why do I tolerate this shabby treatment?"

"I'm a crazy bitch and you love me. Now shut up." She silenced his tongue with hers and shoved him towards the stairs. "I forgot your fucking gum. But get me out of this dress and into bed... I'll make you forget you ever wanted anything but me."

Stacy jolted awake, muscles clenched in a giant knot. A final tremor blew through her big toe and her foot jerked, stopped by the sheet tied around her ankle and twisted around the footboard spindle.

As the twitching abated, she lay in a Schrödinger limbo, asleep and awake, watching the swollen moon paint a ladder on the far wall through the blind slats.

"Dale," she croaked, sandpaper tongue stripping the skin from the top of her mouth. "Be a dear and grab me a glass of water. And a couple of Advil."

He didn't reply. Dead to the world. Not surprising; they'd been animals, going at it until Dale's black chunky lungs nearly collapsed and a chair splintered apart beneath them. Lately their sex life had been... well, non-existent. Since Dale quit smoking, since her work got busier, he'd been in withdrawal, and she'd been moody. Maybe things were turning around.

"Dale, wake up." She flung her arm to his side of the bed, finding only his pillow, damp and sticky. Damn, he probably went downstairs to kill a nicotine urge with a vegan indulgence. "Hey Alexa, turn on the damn light."

The light snapped on. She ground a knuckle into a half-blind eye and saw the blood coating her hand. Her gaze travelled down her crimson smeared arm, across her gore splattered torso, and matted pubic hair. Blood saturated the eggshell sheets, and a lagoon of red collected in the familiar Dale-shaped depression in the mattress.

Stacy shoved herself onto her elbows and saw blood splashed across the wall above the broken chair, tailing all the way to the full-length mirror propped next to the closet. Dale. She wanted to scream but rolled off the bed instead, tearing herself from the clotting mess and staggering to her feet. Only then did she notice the knife in her hand. The largest blade in the block.

The song began again, a diminished chord, quiet and far away, as though following her into this world from a nightmare. Tugging on a nightshirt, she caught her reflection in the mirror, face smeared in blood, eyes wild, earrings glinting a deep purple. His thoughtful gift. Her unique chemistry.

She inched into the hallway and down the stairs, letting the music pull her along.

"Dale?" she whimpered, desperate to hear his voice. It wasn't possible. People didn't black out and kill their husbands. And not just kill. Was there even a word for the mess in the bedroom? No body. But so much blood. No one could survive.

The song crescendoed. That same damn song, coming from the front door. That was it. The video doorbell Dale just installed, badly. Crooked and off center, it churned out a warped melody, as if the batteries were dying. She wiped a hand across her nightshirt, and tapped the console next to the door, watching the video screen resolve.

"Mrs. Todd?" Stacy hid the cleaver behind her back as she opened the door. A rich floral perfume rode in on the night air.

"I heard screaming," drawled the elegant woman, standing on the porch in a pair of men's style pajamas that couldn't hide her curves. She held a leash in one manicured hand and a long skinny cigarette in the other. "Is there a problem?"

Stacy's mind raced. The dog quivered and barked. Was there a problem? Dale was gone. That was a problem. Blood everywhere. That was a problem. Chatting up the sexy old neighbor, with a knife in her hand. A knife that felt natural, like she'd been holding it all her life. That was a definite problem. And all she could think to say was, "You smoke?"

Mrs. Todd shrugged. "Virginia Slims, baby. I quit years ago, but every now and then, in the middle of the night..." Mrs. Todd took a graceful drag and exhaled a perfect stream of carcinogenic fog. "And you didn't answer my question. Is there a problem here?"

The dog barked again, cocking its head as if listening for something. And there it was again. The music.

"I said, is there a problem?" Mrs. Todd repeated, sounding more and more like her shrill little mutt. "Do we need to call the authorities?"

The dog barked. Music drilled into her ears. "No, no problem."

"Then you can't go making such a racket. This is a good neighborhood."

Stacy noticed the smudged wing of Mrs. Todd's eyeliner, and her smeared iridescent pink lipstick. Even doing naked bathroom yoga, Stacy had never seen her neighbor in less than an impeccable full face. To see it melting off like a mask... that was a problem.

The dog barked; the music chimed.

"You look a tad hysterical, hon." Mrs. Todd discharged more smoke into Stacy's face. "Maybe I should speak to the man of the house?"

Stacy's hand tightened on the knife as Mrs. Todd pushed on the door.

"Well, shit." Stacy took in the re-organized remains of Mrs. Todd, identifiable only by the odd wisp of expensively highlighted hair, smoky perfume, and the leash trailing out to a content Bichon still sitting on the porch, lapping blood off one dainty paw. Quite a mess. How on earth was this happening? The dog barked as the droning chimes started again.

"You hear that, right?" Stacy used her forearm to wipe a fresh coat of viscera off her face.

That music. It got into her head. Made her do things. Every time she heard it, her brain itched and her belly felt like a paper nest full of wasps. The dog barked and trotted to the edge of the sidewalk, searching. The song trilled and the dog took off at a dead sprint.

"Wait!" Stacy yelled, chasing after it. She'd find the music. She'd make it stop. She wasn't a killer. She wasn't *hysterical*. She wasn't crazy.

Tendrils of mist snaked through the river bottom neighbourhood, filling low spots and curling around the sodium faux gaslights meant to give Tower Park Mews class. Though in the harsh light of day they looked rusted and tacky.

Music warbled, fading in and out as Stacy ran down the empty street, past Mrs. Todd's house, and the vacant place where that sweet autistic man used to live. She stopped when she reached the small traffic circle, the dog nowhere to be seen.

"Fuck."

She sat on a damp decorative boulder and caught her breath, shivering as the long t-shirt she'd tossed on grew clammy in the wet fog. Where had the little bastard gone? She needed to find it, visit one of her dooms upon it, no joke this time. After it lead her to the music, of course. She held her breath, straining to determine which direction the melody came from.

Everywhere? Nowhere?

Getting closer again. That much she knew for sure. Her head ached and her stomach hurt. That damn tea. The melody faded under the growl of an engine and the crunch of tires. Glaring headlights cut through the mist. Stacey lurched to her feet and ran, slipping on wet grass, knife flying from her hand. The truck squealed to a stop as she staggered into the road.

The engine slowed to an idle, music morphing into a grim calliope tune. Had that always been Mister Softee's ice cream truck jingle?

The driver's side window cranked open and a head poked out. "Hello, ma'am. Could I interest you in some frozen treats?"

Stacy stumbled around to the side of the truck, eyeing the glowing ice cream cones and peeling decals depicting anamorphic sundaes and phallic popsicles. Her stomach gurgled.

"I'll take that as a yes."

"What the hell are you doing here at 2 a.m.?"

"Hold on," he said, slipping into the back and pushing open the serving window. He leaned over the counter, now garbed in paper hat, apron, and a swirly soft serve tie. "Alright, what can I get you?" he asked, waving an ice cream scoop at her. "Dirty Fudge? Cherry Sin-a-bun?"

"Can… you turn that music off?"

He cocked his head and stared at her breasts. "You look like the sort of woman that would enjoy our Monkey Nuts vegan option. And I hope you don't mind me saying so, but you'd definitely appreciate the reduced calories."

Stacy dropped the ice cream scoop, listened to it clank, and watched the eyeball flop onto the pavement.

Damn it.

She wiped her hands on the soft serve tie still hanging over the counter. At some point the music died, along with the truck. It sat there, hulking and quiet, tamed into submission. Her anger faded, her head cleared. What the hell was she doing? She stared at her crusty hands and heard a dog bark.

The barking bounced around the crescent of English village-esque houses that couldn't decide on an architectural influence and as such were a horrendous Tudor, Victorian, Gothic, and Edwardian mashup of steeply pitched rooflines, scrollwork, church windows, and ornamental shutters. All of it a façade. What could else could you expect from a Factory town? Ankle-deep in fog, Stacy stomped barefoot along the asphalt, gagging on the reek of cooling innards. The ice cream man, Mrs. Todd... Dale. She wasn't capable of it. She wasn't crazy.

"Then where the hell is everybody?" she muttered.

The barking led her into an outdoor square with a gazebo, sprawling gardens, and sculpted topiaries like alien landscapes in the dark. Another bark and she spotted a flash of white fuzz darting between thorny rose bushes and a wheelbarrow full of mulch.

Stacy chased, but lost the dog again when she tripped over a rake and crashed through the bushes, smacking her face against the mucky earth.

"Goddamnit," she groaned, spitting dirt. A stench sailed into her nose and she rolled away from a modest pile of dog shit she'd nearly face planted in. Jesus, couldn't people pick up after their animals? The thought dwindled as next to the canine feces she noticed a collection of cigarette butts. Virginia Slims, filters smudged with shimmering lipstick.

Dale would speak up and tell Mrs. Todd to scoop up after her dog and stop using the square as her personal ashtray. When Dale had a problem, he dealt with it. He'd deal with Mrs. Todd. He always dealt with Mrs. Todd.

"I'll handle it, Stace. Let me talk to her—" Her throat closed over the words. Dale was gone. She'd woken up in a pool of blood with a knife in her hand. Dale, his body, was gone.

"I'm sorry." Tears streaked through the gore on her cheeks and her stomach knotted as she sobbed, crawling across bicycle tire ruts and onto the concrete slab under the gazebo where she huddled in a ball beside a wrought iron bench, rocking back and forth. "I didn't mean to." She spotted another cigarette butt on the concrete, not a Virginia Slim, no lipstick. Just a tiny little Camel.

The unnerving tritone rang out again. Stacy clapped her hands over her ears, but the song kept going, sawing back and forth across the grain of her sanity.

Closer. Louder.

A bicycle whipped into the square, sailing along the paths, circling the gazebo. A kid from the look of it. A kid up way past his bed time. Big headphones over his shaggy mop, and his music relentlessly leaking around them. That song. Stacy wanted to bury her head in the ground and suffocate. The kid circled and circled. Faster, closer, louder. And the next time he flew by, he flipped her the bird.

"I'm. Not. Crazy!" Stacy screamed, scuttling out of the gazebo and grabbing the rake.

"What the absolute hell," said Dale from the front foyer. "Do we even own a rake?"

Stacy stopped shovelling soiled clothing into the washing machine. Dale? She held her breath. Listened to the rasp of metal on metal, a sharp counterpoint to garbled notes stinging the dead air.

A number of muttered "for fuck's sake," followed, punching her in the gut, expelling the held breath. Dale. She steadied herself against the ironing board and stepped into the kitchen. Her dishevelled husband stood in the opposite doorway wrestling with the front wheel of his bike, its spokes twisted around a rusty rake head sporting two feet of shattered handle.

They stared at each other.

"Thank god," moaned Stacy, rushing over and burying her head against his chest, sandwiching the mangled bike. She caught the scent of cigarettes and something darkly floral. "I thought you..." She jammed the back of her hand against her running nose. Sniffled.

Dale leaned the rake infested tire against the wall. "And what did my ice cream ever do to you?" Stacy glanced over at the smashed cartons, oozing across the kitchen table. Dale picked up the scoop from the tile floor. "You're crazy, you know."

"I'm not..." She turned her back on him and walked to the sink, ran her finger across the empty slot in the knife block, and jammed her hands into the hot soapy water.

"And you're missing an earring. What have you been doing?"

She felt her ear and sure enough the right bauble was gone. Shit. She must have lost it in the square or when she was pulling her clothes off in the laundry room. Tears stung her eyes. A thoughtful gift. Reacting to her unique chemistry. She promised never to take them off. "Dale, I'm so sorry — wait." She turned to face him. "Where the hell were you? What happened? I thought I'd... there was so much blood."

"Right?" he laughed. "I almost had a heart attack when I got up to take a leak. You might've at least warned me. Explains your weird mood anyway."

It dawned on her. The squeezing fist in her belly, the vague dampness between her legs. She laughed, a thin hysterical wail.

"After I cleaned up, I was wide awake and jonesing like you wouldn't believe, so I went for a walk."

"You went out for cigarettes?" she cried. "I thought I'd *murdered* you."

"I smoked one and threw away the rest. Jesus, calm down," he said flopping onto the couch. "Anyway, you did murder my bike."

"The music made me."

"Music?" Dale gave her a queer look and took out his phone, frowning at it before putting it back in his pocket. "Seriously, do you hear yourself?"

"No, it's real. It—" A bark cut through her protest and she turned back to the window. "That god damn dog is shitting on our lawn again."

Illuminated by a fakey yellow gaslight, the Bichon raked a marigold with its muddy back feet. "I'm going to execute that little beast."

Dale yawned. "Feed it to an alligator."

"Strangle it with a string of Christmas lights."

"Bury it in a shallow grave."

"Mmm…" Her left ear itched like mad as the dark dissonant melody once again started up. She clawed at her lobe, ripping out the remaining earring. The stud sat in her palm, now a deep red and faintly, but definitely, chiming. Unique chemistry. A song of unraveling. Sending her on a tour of violent idiocy. Such a thoughtful gift. So thoughtful Dale never would have thought of it on his own. He needed a woman's advice. A lonely widow. Naked yoga in the morning. Smeared makeup at night. A husband who went insane…

"In the gazebo?" Stacy asked.

"Huh?"

"The gazebo in the square. Is that where you go to smoke at night?" She plunged the earring into the water as Dale joined her by the sink and peered into the yard.

"Uh, Stace?"

Rake ruined bike.

"Yes, Dale?"

Bludgeoned vegan ice cream.

"Where's Mrs. Todd?"

Stacy curled her fingers around the knife handle beneath the suds as the dog trotted down the street, all alone, dragging its leash behind.

Happy Ending

Sarah L. Johnson

Open your eyes... eyes you don't remember closing. Though they did close, at some point. Something closed them. At some point. And you went somewhere. Away. Now you're awake in absolute darkness, cold like a dull set of teeth chewing through your body heat. And speaking of body, an experimental wriggle confirms you are whole and typically configured. Except your knuckles knock against an unyielding barrier at your sides. You've barely raised your head when it cracks against the ceiling, and your elbows dig into the floor.

A box.

The muffled acoustics are all the proof you need and your nerves catch fire in a frenzy of cramps and sweat and sour gulps, pummelling the roof and sides of your prison, heels hammering the floor in flattened thumps, thrashing your head side to side until you're dizzy and dry heaving.

Don't scream.

The air in this box is all you have. How long will air hold out underground? How long have you been here? Too long. The air is already gone, your lungs are overstuffed vacuum canisters sucking honey through a cocktail straw and you can't breathe you can't breathe, you can't...

Slow down, slow down. You're using it all. Too quickly. Metabolism. And it's not lack of oxygen that gets you, it's carbon dioxide turning your blood to acid. Visualize. It's not a slab two inches above your nose but the open sky full of galaxies circling like wild animals and so... much... space. Expanding. Your body-mind quiets and you're on a moonlit hilltop, a raft on the ocean, the Factory floor, gazing up at a pigeon's nest you must have seen or at least known about, at some point. You're fine. You're okay. You're calm.

You're completely fucked.

An impossible mistake, yet here you are. You scratch at the smooth hard material to the sides, above, and below. No texture, grain, seams, or irregularities. Like glass, or concrete. You don't want to touch it anymore. So you walk your fingers over whatever skin you can reach, chest, belly, legs, and finally lingering on the fuzz at your groin. You are uninjured as far as you can tell. And naked. In a box. Which seems weird. Less and less like a mistake.

At least you can move, a little. You can touch your own body, and honestly that's preferable to the claustrophobic walls of your... you don't dare even think the word. Who did this? Management? Corporate? Does it matter? The Factory has a way of getting people right where They want them. Remaining calm is easier this time, aided by the meditative act of combing your cold fingers through your pubic hair. The area soft and warm. Proof you are still alive.

And that, is a kind of pleasure.

You spread your legs wide as you can, which isn't wide at all, but nevertheless helps with the mood. Tender flesh reacts to your practiced touch. At some point, muscle memory takes over. This feeling is all life has left you, and it becomes your entire life. A universe expanding from singularity.

Born with a bang.

Spasms of wet heat leave your body even as they draw you one gasp closer to your last. Dirty air fouls your lungs but you suck it back, because what choice do you have, for as long as you have? You breathe and stroke and thrust and clench. Thighs tremble and the soles of your feet burn, but you're close. Rising, cresting, releasing, falling. Panting in your tomb until you can begin once more.

Again. And again.

Until you're too weak to continue with your numb fingers. Your eyes close and sink like lead into the dim pillow of your brain. Down and away. Heat death creeps under your skin, nuzzling your insteps, kissing behind your knees, licking between your thighs, and at some point...

Finishing you off.

Insatiable

Solomon Black

Golden mane, golden curls.

Catching the wind, rustling, impatient.

Writhing.

But there is no wind.

Just curls, coiling, uncoiling.

Twisted, hungry.

So hungry.

Always hungry.

For bones, and blood, and souls.

Medusa, Stheno, and Euryale.

Straining for love, restless, anxious.

Slithering.

But there is no love.

Just men, heroic, common.

Fearful, angry.

So angry.

Always angry.

At everything, and everyone, and themselves.

Perseus.

Sandals, Sword, Helm.

Gifts from the gods.

Scheming gods, vengeful gods.

Nothing is free, nothing can be.

Your shield will not save you from the wind.

From anger.

From love.

From those hungry curls.

Nothing can.

Purgatorio Towers Gazette

Social Committee

Calling for volunteers to plan the winter solstice party, specifically to coordinate the following:

- Midnight Bloodening
- Feast on the Flesh of the Wicked
- Interment of the Night Blooming Tulip bulb (since the vernal equinox was more or less a disaster, not to name names)

Please contact **Brenda** at contact@the-seventh-terrace.com **by email only** as she would remind us all how much she hates it when you knock on the aquarium glass.

The Winnebago Club

Last Wednesday of the month in the basement commons, in spite of the banging and screaming coming from under the concrete floor, which is now reported to have dissipated and indeed never to have existed in the first place. This month's subject of discussion is the D-23 Chieftain (pdf blue prints attached).

Cookbook Fundraiser

The rumors are true! Terrace VI is in the planning stages of improved feasting facilities and an expanded vomitorium. To fund this remodel, the Gluttons are putting together a Taste of Purgatory Cookbook. Submit your most disturbing recipes to **Gary** at contact@the-seventh-terrace.com

Special Announcements

The slime in the West elevator bank has receded. After 40 days and 40 nights of truly prodigious production, the Hagfish was retrieved from the elevator shaft and the cars are now in working order. Though it should be noted that risk of mirror spiders is ongoing.

Roy, from Terrace III has submitted an official grievance against the residents of Terrace IV regarding their failure to properly sort organics and recyclables. If the situation is not rectified, he "will fucking gut you, you lazy pigs". Tenant's Association President, Gary, reminds residents to properly sort their organics and recyclables according to the colour coded bins now located at the morning lava ponds.

Factory Overstock Sale!

Blue Jelly Clots in every species. Limited quantities. Rock bottom prices. Perfect gift for toy collectors.

Memorial Service

It is with heavy hearts we announce the passing our dear friend Mr. Todd. You knew him, of course, as the kindly elder groundskeeper, keeping the shrubs trimmed and bushes lurked. Why, you may ask, given our strict policy of not hiring external contractors and our repeated attempts to run him off? A question with no answer, but his efforts were acceptably sinister.

As many of you already know, or suspected, Mr. Todd departed this mortal coil for parts unknown after an encounter with a Winnebago door while cycling along Highway 80. He is survived by his wife of indeterminate years (and timeless ass), three ungrateful children, and seven worthless grandchildren.

The traditional Arby's meatcraft gorging will be held in Sub-basement Social Hall C following the service. The slothful should make an effort to arrive early, before the gluttons.

Personals

Personal shoppers wanted, contact the Factory... Must have reliable transportation

Ahimsa Lotus Garden is looking for a new Manager.

Skin Deep is a wholly owned subsidiary of Monster Matchmaking, a Factory owned and operated personal services corporation.

Fully tanned and cured incel hides, two for one, OBO.

Lost & Found

- Red Ribbon
- Semi-autonomous Tentacle
- 437 Orphaned Mittens and counting
- Pair of Noise Cancelling Headphones
- Memory Foam Mattress (memories included)
- Magic 8-Ball
- A Foot

Funnies

KNOCK KNOCK

who's there?

ICE CREAM

ice cream who?

ICE CREAM IF YOU DON'T LET ME INSIDE

…

…

we're all screaming on the inside

MENTIONS

Are we thankful? Meh. Sadly, the sort of things we're thankful for can't be thrust upon the world until after the statute of limitations has passed, or we're dead, or both. Though in the meantime, we can grudgingly offer what passes for monstrous heartfelt gratitude.

In no particular order, we'd like to thank our friends and families. Particularly the endless (albeit confused and strained) patience of Spousal Units. Emily and Aaron for their fabulous cover and graphics, the YA section, Dante Alighieri, various Fish Creek parking lots, under bridges, Frankie the Duck, and of course Arby's.

Last, but not least, we wouldn't even be writing this with without our patrons gods, watching over us from their exile in Purgatory Starbucks, nursing their dark roasts, whispering secrets into our shared plasmodium.

And to anyone who even vaguely encouraged us to run with a bad idea, we thank you, and we'll see you in Purgatory. You know what you did.

ABOUT THE AUTHORS

Photo Credit: Todd Kuipers

Robert Bose has a fondness for tentacles, picnics, absolute darkness, exotic Gin and stylish Bourbon, not necessarily in that order. He's the editor of a variety of books and anthologies for Coffin Hop Press and the author of myriad short stories including the fiendish collection, Fishing with the Devil. When not writing, editing, publishing and running unfathomable distances, he spends his time annoying his wife, pestering his troublesome children, and working as a Director of R&D for an trendy software company you've hopefully never heard of.

Find him online at www.robertbose.com

Photo Credit: Jodi O.

Sarah L. Johnson is a curly hair gladiator, ultra marathoner, literary events wrangler, and misfit fictioneer. Her stories have appeared in Room Magazine, Plenitude, On Spec, Shock Totem, Crossed Genres, *Year's Best Hardcore Horror Vol. 2* (Red Room Press), and the Bram Stoker Award nominated *Dark Visions 1* (Grey Matter Press). She's the author of *Suicide Stitch: Eleven Tales* (EMP Publishing) and the blasphemous apocalyptic thriller, *Infractus* (Coffin Hop Press).

Find her online at www.sarahljohnson.com

Made in the USA
Las Vegas, NV
07 May 2022

ALSO BY SOFI LAPORTE